As His Lips Touched Hers,

she placed one hand on his cheek, her fingers searching out the strong line of his jaw. The kiss was deep and strong, and the fire that had been waiting to be lit was ignited. His arm went around her slender waist, pulling her close. They both surrendered to the moment, neither wanting to break away.

When finally, reluctantly, Gus drew back, his eyes were fond and loving. She looked down at her hand in his, and knew at that moment, all warnings aside, that she had met a man she could lose her heart to.

SUZANNE MICHELLE

likes to think that she finds romance in her own backyard. Living in Houston with an extended family that includes four children, she loves to write and always uses a purple pen.

Dear Reader:

SILHOUETTE DESIRE is an exciting new line of contemporary romances from Silhouette Books. During the past year, many Silhouette readers have written in telling us what other types of stories they'd like to read from Silhouette, and we've kept these comments and suggestions in mind in developing SILHOUETTE DESIRE.

DESIREs feature all of the elements you like to see in a romance, plus a more sensual, provocative story. So if you want to experience all the excitement, passion and joy of falling in love, then SILHOUETTE DESIRE is for you.

Karen Solem
Editor-in-Chief
Silhouette Books

SUZANNE MICHELLE
Forbidden Melody

Silhouette Desire
Published by Silhouette Books New York

America's Publisher of Contemporary Romance

SILHOUETTE BOOKS, a Division of Simon & Schuster, Inc.
1230 Avenue of the Americas, New York, N.Y. 10020

Distributed by Pocket Books

ISBN: 0-671-49570-4

First Silhouette Books printing November, 1984

10 9 8 7 6 5 4 3 2 1

Books by Suzanne Michelle

Silhouette Desire

Forbidden
Melody

1

A brass fanfare rang out through the star-filled night and was answered by the brilliant burst of the string choir, the sonorous rhythms of the kettle-drums, the crash of cymbals. The beautiful conductor, coaxing the noisy melodies of Tchaikovsky's *1812* Overture, held out her arms to the orchestra; her gray eyes flashed triumphantly as the music reached a crescendo, peaked, then fell softly to a whisper. Madeline Mark held the symphony in the palm of her slender hands, no less powerful for their delicacy, no less sure for their gracefulness, and the festive crowd fell under her spell as had the musicians on stage.

Before the concert began, the new conductor, resplendent in a black tuxedo, her long hair in braids curled around her head, a string of pearls twisted through the silken black tresses, had slipped out the door of her dressing room. She stood in the shadow of a small clump of trees close to the Miller Theater stage. With her hand, she shielded her eyes from the late afternoon sun and watched the crowd gather. Forty thousand people were spreading out their blankets on the hill in Hermann Park. They came early for the best seats. They brought fried chicken and Frisbees, cold white wine, radios, poorboys and lemonade. They came as they did every year to celebrate the Fourth of July. The hot summer night was usually predictable; the music was an accompaniment to the fireworks that followed.

Not this year, she thought to herself, her chin set with determination. This year was different. This year there was a new conductor. This year, she vowed, rubbing one fist in the palm of her other hand, she'd give the city of Houston a concert to remember. This year, they'd remember, Madeline Mark came to town.

The orange sun ducked behind the big city skyline. The crowd settled back for the free concert. The lights were dimmed and an expectant hush fell over the audience. From the start, the tall, slender conductor had her way. She knew what she was doing and she loved every minute of it. With poise and quiet dignity, she set the tempo and maintained the rhythm, playing the orchestra as if it were the greatest of all instruments and she alone knew the score. From her baton, from the tips of her fingers, from the depths of her heart and soul flowed a fierce inner light that gave shape to the music. She stretched out her hand and she was obeyed. Her nod, her softest gesture, her slightest glance, were law, and more than one hundred musicians gladly bent their wills to match hers.

By the time the cannons on either side of the outdoor stage exploded like giant sparklers, signaling the start of fireworks, Madeline Mark had won over the hearts of audience and musicians alike. The whine of skyrockets soared above the music, and high in the sky, Roman candles and bottle rockets spewed and crackled. Green and red and blue they broke against the night, held fast for a moment, then began to fall in showers of gold and silver. Madeline Mark was no less dazzling. It was her night, her celebration, her victory.

When she closed the concert with "The Battle Hymn of the Republic" and "The Yellow Rose of Texas," the delighted audience leapt to their feet, giving their new conductor a resounding ovation. The excited crowd didn't want to let her go, and time after time she came back to center stage, always including the orchestra in her elegant bow, her eyes shining, her smile radiant. Finally, blowing a kiss to the musicians, she left the stage for good, tired but happy.

"Markey—you were wonderful." Brew Baker's voice boomed as he welcomed Madeline backstage with outstretched arms. The distinguished symphony business manager had long arms and a portly midriff and wore a three-piece pinstriped suit. A white carnation was pinned to the lapel of his jacket, and his dark silk tie was perpetually askew. "They simply adored you!"

Flushed with success, Madeline grinned at the exuberant spirits of the administrator. She was hot, and wisps of her hair curled in the tiny beads of dampness glistening on her forehead. "Do you really think so?" she asked breathlessly. Being the first woman—and the youngest—to conduct the Metropolitan Symphony was no small challenge, and Madeline was acutely conscious of the work she had cut out for her. She was not intimidated by the challenge but neither was she unmindful of it. It was essential that the public like her.

"I know so," Brew answered with conviction. He was beaming his approval as he shook her hand. "I've never seen anything like it. What drama, what style—you had them eating out of your hand!"

"It was a good show, wasn't it," Madeline said simply, her long black lashes closing momentarily over her gray eyes as she took a deep breath. She was still intoxicated with the magic and excitement of the night. She loved music. She loved a good show. Both had been spectacular and she knew it. Taking over the reins of any orchestra, especially one as highly regarded as this one, was a big task. The audience had been filled with many who were waiting to see whether or not she deserved the responsibility.

Shaking free of her reverie, Madeline returned to the present. There was no time for contemplation. Now the members of the orchestra were filing backstage and, of one accord, they surrounded her with reserved, almost shy congratulations. They had been working with their new conductor now for more than a month and their respect for her talent and position was evident in their praise.

"That was wonderful, Ms. Mark!" a small, vivacious blonde said, her short hair curling naturally around her face in a halo soft as cotton candy.

Emily Jane, a gifted harpist, was ten years younger than Madeline. Her blue eyes were wide with admiration and it was clear that she idolized her new conductor.

"So were you." Madeline returned the compliment with genuine pleasure. She gave the younger woman an affectionate smile. "Now I know why they call you Angel."

"If only we could keep her feet on the ground," Figaro McPhee teased the young harpist. The swarthy first violinist was vigorously pumping Madeline's arm, her small hand clutched in both of his. His black wiry hair stood out from his head, and his bushy eyebrows moved up and down as he spoke. ". . . and her head out of the clouds."

"Oh, Figaro, you're one to talk!" Angel retorted with a blush. "Winking at me during the national anthem." She shook her pretty blond head at the older man.

Madeline laughed good-naturedly—and a bit wistfully—at the easy camaraderie of the other musicians. Most of them had known each other for a long time, and they obviously liked each other. Madeline was still the newcomer, and though she knew it was important that she establish herself as their conductor, not as a pal, she envied their easy relationships and couldn't help wishing she didn't have to remain apart from the group. But she did, she reminded herself. It came with the job. Her reply was warm but businesslike. "That was a splendid solo in the first movement," she said to her concertmaster.

"I was only following your brilliant instructions," Figaro answered gallantly. He bent to kiss her hand in a flamboyant gesture, the heritage of an Italian mother and Irish father. Then he stood up, his dark eyes filled with real pride. "You stole the show tonight. Congratulations from all of us."

"She certainly did," was an immediate reply from across Figaro's shoulders. "But we want a chance to congratulate our new conductor ourselves, if you don't mind, Mr. McPhee." With that lighthearted warning, Thomas Richards Duncan stepped forward, pushing the concertmaster aside in a jocular manner.

"Thank you, T.R." Madeline shook hands with the short, chubby percussionist. "You didn't do such a bad job yourself. That finale was superb."

T.R. grinned, basking in the praise. His thick rimless glasses were slipping down his nose. Of all the members of the orchestra, he seemed to be the least intimidated by the conductor. In fact, there seemed to be very little that intimidated T.R. "And how about that last roll? Was I great or was I great?" He put his thumbs in the crooks of his arms, preening for the enthusiastic applause that followed.

In spite of herself, Madeline found T.R.'s informality a pleasant relief and understood somehow that it was not due to a lack of respect. But as she joined in the round of applause, Madeline spotted out of the corner of her eye a solitary figure at the back of the hall, and a slight frown creased her forehead. Maurice Spender, a brilliant young flutist, was quietly slipping out the side door toward the dressing rooms. So, Madeline thought to herself as she saw him leave, even a good show isn't enough to jolt him out of his problems. She was worried about the troubled young man. He had come in late for the performance, almost missing the curtain, and he'd missed a couple of cues in the second movement. His attention during rehearsals for the past few weeks hadn't been much better. Figaro had told her the boy was having romantic problems, he thought, but Madeline was sure it was more than just being in love. Maurice was one of the most promising flutists in the country, and Madeline knew she had to handle the situation carefully. She wanted to help the talented musician but she also had to do what was best for the orchestra as a whole.

She would have to get to the bottom of it, she promised herself as the adoring throng captured her attention once again. She couldn't help smiling at the high spirits of the group and was glad that Maurice seemed one of a kind.

"That's enough for one night," Brew Baker was saying with authority. "Ms. Mark's got work to do, I'm afraid." He had made his way through the crowd and reclaimed his place at Madeline's side.

"And that goes for you, too," Madeline said to the orchestra. She raised one hand to get their attention. "We have a new season to get ready for—and a European tour. I'll see you in the morning, nine o'clock sharp."

The musicians groaned together in mock despair. "Nine o'clock! That's the crack of dawn."

Madeline grinned, for once letting her guard down. It was, after all, a natural protest. "Okay. Make that two o'clock. I'll give you a couple of hours off for the Fourth of July."

With exaggerated sighs of relief, the musicians

began putting away their instruments and gathering up their belongings. Madeline turned to Brew, her hands on her hips. "Now what's this about more work? I thought we were going to a party."

Brew took her by the elbow and they headed for her dressing room. "That's right, we are, but I think you're going to find it seems a whole lot like work. When Mamie Spencer gives a party you can bet your bottom dollar she's got something up her sleeve."

"What do you mean?" Madeline was curious. Mamie Spencer was president of the symphony board. "I've heard good things about her and she seemed nice enough when I met her."

"Whatever you heard, you heard right," Brew continued with obvious admiration. "As far as Houston's concerned, she's the grand lady of music. It's just that she's got more ideas than I can keep up with." He shook his head. "One scheme after another. She never runs dry."

"I'm looking forward to seeing her again," Madeline said with genuine pleasure. "If she's a human dynamo, that's exactly what we need around here, especially if we're going to pull together a tour abroad this year." Madeline stopped at the door to her dressing room.

"Well, if anyone can keep up with Mamie, you're the one to do it," Brew said with a confident laugh. "The two of you just might pull it off. No one else would even try."

Madeline had an earnest look in her eyes. "Well, it's not something I like doing on such short notice, but since Otto had already scheduled the time, I think we need to put our heads together and try to pull this thing out of the fire. It can put Houston on the map for good." Her predecessor, Otto Braun, had been a man of great vision as well as a fine musician. He had been a popular conductor, and Madeline knew she had some big shoes to fill in taking over his job. The European tour was an important obligation, and though she would have preferred to wait another year, she was willing to see it through to the end.

"I know," Brew agreed wholeheartedly. "Otto thought so too. So does Mamie. In fact, we all do. It's just that with Otto's death, the fund-raising plans had to be pushed aside. First things first, and hiring a new conductor was first." Brew folded his arms across his chest. Thinking back over the past seemed to make him glum.

"Don't worry," Madeline said, giving him a reassuring pat on the shoulder. "We'll find the money. You'll see." Sensing that the older man needed a respite from administrative problems, she decided to change the subject. "Now don't you think it's about time to turn off the lights and lock up? After all, it is the Fourth of July—time for a celebration."

Brew's face brightened at the thought of the approaching party. He looked around at the deserted stage. "You bet—but don't worry about the lights. The one thing you don't have to do around here is close up shop." He turned to go, then remembered something. "You still have the directions I gave you this morning, don't you?"

Madeline had opened the door to her dressing

room and was standing with her hand on the doorknob. "Yes. I'm just going to slip in here and pick up my purse. Then I'm off."

"You're sure you don't want me to take you?" Brew seemed unconvinced.

"I'm sure," Madeline said with a certain finality. They had been all through this before. "I need to find my own way around Houston. You've been great but I can't always have someone drive me around. After all, I've been here for six weeks."

"Okay." Brew threw up his hands in a friendly gesture. "See you later."

"You bet." And with that final word, Madeline was in the privacy of her small, unadorned dressing room, alone at last. It had been a good evening, and without realizing it, she was humming a bar of "The Eyes of Texas." Already she was beginning to feel like she belonged to this place. Her father was a diplomat, and as a child, she had traveled all over the world. As a result, she never felt a stranger wherever she was. But, on the other hand, she had never really felt at home anyplace. As she looked around the tiny cubicle that had been given her, at the small wooden table with the oval mirror hanging above it, at the dusty show bills plastered on the bare walls, she felt a surge of affection rush through her. She knew that she was falling in love with Houston. Already it seemed like home.

She bent to study her face in the mirror. "You did all right, girl," she said softly to herself in an imitation Texas drawl. "You've still got a few mountains to move, so don't get cocky!" She raised a stern finger to her reflection. Then, quickly touching up her makeup and putting on some fresh lipstick, she hurried to gather up her things.

As she made her way through the building, she impulsively decided to take the stage exit. The night air was clear and the park nearly empty of the crowd that had been here a little while ago. Paper cups and empty popcorn sacks were the only reminders of her triumph, and as she stood in center of the stage, the memory of the music was a sweet echo to her ears. Music was her life, her first love. It had been the only stable thing in a childhood that knew no other constants. Beethoven was the same whether she lived in England or Germany. Chopin and Wagner knew no national boundaries. Her parents, though devoted and loving, were often preoccupied with their many duties, and Markey had made a world for herself at the piano where she was never lonely, never a foreigner. Music became her solace, a buffer from the realities of a complicated world. As a little girl, she had dreamed of one day conducting her own orchestra and now that that dream had come true, Madeline could scarcely believe her good fortune. She had been an assistant conductor under Sarah Caldwell in Boston before coming to Houston. This job was the dream of a lifetime, and nothing was more important to her. Nothing. She had every intention of being the best conductor the Metropolitan Symphony had ever had.

"Night, Ms. Mark," a young stagehand called out as he walked across the back of the stage, switching off the lights. "Sure was a good show."

"Thanks," Madeline said, coming out of her

reverie. "Thanks a lot." Straightening her shoulders, she sighed softly, realizing for the first time how tired she was. She had given everything she had to the evening's performance and now felt drained. She looked across the park to the high-rise condominium where she lived. A light was on in the bedroom, and for a moment she was tempted to go home, kick off her shoes and read a good book. Tomorrow night, she promised herself, I'll save that for tomorrow. Throwing her bag over her shoulder, she headed for her white BMW. She had come early and was parked close to the stage. As she started the powerful engine and turned toward River Oaks, she thought ahead to the party. The invitation had come at the last minute. Mamie had said when she called that a few of her friends were dropping over after the concert and she hoped Madeline would join them. Madeline had been delighted to accept. She had already met several board members but she was looking forward to getting to know them better. She could use all the help she could get in the year ahead.

Pulling up in front of the elegant Spanish-style mansion where Mamie Spencer lived, Madeline parked her car on the far side of the driveway, behind a Checker cab that had been painted red. The yard and porch were lit with gaslights that lined the circular driveway, and there was an air of graciousness about the carefully landscaped yard. The two-story house was a pale pink stucco; the tiled roof a darker red. Through the undraped front windows, Madeline could see the guests clustered in small groups, chatting, smiling, enjoying themselves.

Madeline started up the front walk, stopping for a moment to look up at the sky. The lights of the city seemed far away in this secluded neighborhood and she welcomed the peaceful solitude. Suddenly, out of nowhere, a falling star streaked across the darkness and Madeline drew her breath in sharply. She had never seen anything so beautiful.

"That's always a good omen, don't you think?" asked a deep voice at her elbow.

Startled, Madeline whirled around to see who had spoken and her eyes fell on the most striking man she had ever seen. "I beg your pardon?" she asked, looking up at a tall, slender man in horn-rimmed glasses and dressed in an elegant black tuxedo, a dashing red sash around his waist. There was something special about him, something en-dearing, something very different, and the provoca-tive twinkle in his black eyes seemed to caress her and hold her captive.

"A sign from the heavens, a beautiful woman—all in the same breath. That has to be a good omen." The stranger's voice was intimate and seductive. He had looked her over from head to toe and was quite obviously pleased with what he saw. He didn't wait for her reply but took her instead by the elbow and started toward the big house. "I knew I would like you the minute you stepped out on the stage tonight, but I had no idea you'd be more beautiful up close than you were on the stage. In the distance, you were something of a mirage, too good to be true."

Surprised at the intensity of her own unruly emotions, Madeline struggled to meet the boldness of his black eyes. With a certain coldness in her voice, she said, "That's missing the point, isn't it? It's the music that's important." He had caught her off guard and she had to say something, anything to turn his attention from her. Instinctively, she stiffened as she attempted to regain some control over the situation.

"Oh, that was spectacular, too," the handsome man replied with what seemed like true admiration. "The best. Listening to your sorcery was like falling in love. I may never be the same again." If he had heard the coolness in her voice, he gave no sign of it. He had fallen into step beside her, his long legs easily matching her purposeful stride. "But then that's always the way it is, isn't it? Falling in love turns the world upside down. Nothing is ever the same."

"That's what poets would have us believe," Madeline returned smoothly as she hurried up the steps to the front door. She had never before been so immediately attracted to a man, and she was valiantly trying to sound indifferent. She had no intention of letting him know how close he had come.

"Maybe I should read more poetry," he replied, leaning against the doorjamb. "It's a whole new experience for me." He was apparently in no hurry to go inside.

"A little bit of poetry never hurt anyone," Madeline answered, ignoring the implications of his remark. She was beginning to feel a little trapped, as if he were detaining her. Who did he think he was, anyway? She was starting to fume at his casual arrogance that seemed to assume so much. "Now if you don't mind—" she began. But before she had a chance to finish, the front door was flung open and they were face-to-face with none other than Mamie Spencer herself. She was wearing a long skirt made of three tiers of red, white and blue cotton, and her scooped-neck blouse was white, trimmed with heavy lace.

"Madeline, my dear! It's so good to see you." Mamie's greeting was effusive. It was obvious that she intended to say more when her blue eyes fell on the man leaning against the doorframe. "Well, Gus, I was wondering what had happened to you. I thought you would be here hours ago. I should have known our new conductor wouldn't be so insistent with the bell." She smiled at Madeline.

Madeline looked over at Gus, whoever he was, and saw him pull apologetically away from the doorbell. He looked so surprised that Madeline had to laugh.

"Oh, no," he said, momentarily flustered. It was his turn to be embarrassed, and Madeline was showing no mercy. "My mind was on other things, I guess," he added, his eyes never leaving Madeline's.

"He seems to be easily distracted," Madeline said sweetly. She didn't want him to explain any further so she didn't give him a chance to talk. With a sideways glance at the man next to her, she extended her right hand to her hostess. "It's good to see you again, Mrs. Spencer." Madeline had regained her poise and self-assurance and was giving Mamie her undivided attention.

"I'm so delighted to see you again," Mamie replied, her blue eyes twinkling approval. "The concert tonight was magnificent." She looked first to Madeline, then to Gus. "I am assuming you two have met?"

"Well, not formally," Gus said. "We've rubbed elbows, shall we say, Ms. Mark?"

"Something like that," Madeline replied. What was it about this man that she found so unsettling? she wondered. "I don't believe I got your name," she said offhandedly as she followed Mamie into the spacious entranceway.

"Noble, Gus Noble," he said over her shoulder as he followed the two women into the house. "At your service."

Madeline turned to look at him, her interest suddenly piqued. Her gray eyes opened wide as a look of amazement slowly crossed her face. "You mean Gus Noble, the songwriter?"

"The one and only." He snapped his heels together and bowed slightly. In the bright lights of the house, Gus was even more handsome than he had seemed outside in the shadows. His black hair was tousled and his dark eyes were compelling.

"He's the reason I'm having this little get-together," Mamie said with a confidential air. She took Madeline by the arm and led her toward the living room. "I thought Brewster had told you all about my little plan."

"What little plan?" Brew demanded, as they walked into the living room. "Do I hear you talking about me?"

Mamie looked innocently over at Brew Baker. "Now I'm sure I told you, Brewster. You've just forgotten." She turned to Madeline and explained, "He's got the worst memory of anyone I know."

"Now, Mamie, you know that's not true." Brew

walked over to Madeline and gave her a welcoming smile. "I always remember everything she says. How could I forget, what with her calling me ten times a week?" He gave Madeline a look that clearly said, "See what I told you?"

Mamie sat down in a large wing chair. "Oh, the way you do go on," she said, throwing up her hands helplessly. "Madeline's going to think I'm a terrible busybody." She was obviously quite accustomed to Brew's teasing.

But by this time, Madeline was being greeted by the other guests and it was a few minutes before she could try to find out more about Mamie's "little plan." Gus Noble was standing by the fireplace over at one end of the room, and Madeline was acutely aware of his eyes on her as she made conversation with the other guests. He too had been surrounded by guests and was now talking to a short man with gray hair who was smoking a pipe.

Brew was at her side again after a short absence. "Here you go," he said affably, handing Madeline a glass of champagne. "You must be thirsty after that long performance."

Realizing that she was indeed very thirsty, Madeline responded, "I certainly am." She took a grateful sip; then, taking advantage of the chatter that surrounded her, she murmured, "What's all this about Gus Noble and Mamie?" She smiled graciously at one of the women she had just met, and hoped she hadn't been overheard.

"Your guess is as good as mine," Brew said with a helpless shrug. "But don't say I didn't warn you."

Madeline was about to press for something more

when Mamie struck the side of her wineglass with a spoon, calling for everyone's attention. She was standing next to Gus, who was now leaning against the mantel. "Please let me introduce you all to my friend Gus Noble. Most of you have already met him, and I'm sure you've all heard of him. If you haven't you will." She flashed a smile at Gus.

There was a smattering of polite applause as the guests gathered round. Whatever Mamie had up her sleeve, they were interested.

"Gus is going to make that European tour possible for us," Mamie said with a glowing smile, pausing for the soft *oohs* and *ahs* she knew would follow. She was quite obviously used to being the center of attention, and was fully aware of the drama of the moment. She didn't intend to rush through this instant of glory. "Gus has written the most wonderful symphony for a movie that's going to be made right here in Houston at our new sound studio." She looked over at Gus for information. *"Forbidden Stars*—that's the name of the movie, isn't it?"

Gus nodded, seeming to know that was all the answer Mamie needed. He looked over at Madeline, a slow smile curling his lips.

Mamie turned her attention to the other guests. *"Forbidden Stars*—and the Metropolitan Symphony Orchestra will produce the soundtrack, for no small fee, of course."

Instantly the room was alive with enthusiastic questions. Everyone was bristling with curiosity. Everyone, that is, except Madeline, who had turned pale with fury at the surprise announcement.

"How dare she make decisions without consulting me first!" she whispered urgently to Brew, her gray eyes flashing angrily. She might be young; she might be new; this might be her first orchestra; but she had definite professional standards. "I make all the musical decisions. That's what my contract says."

"When you've known Mamie as long as I have, you'll understand that there's nothing she wouldn't dare." He was speaking softly so as not to be heard. "But don't forget, she has the orchestra's best interests at heart. This could be a great idea." Brew seemed to be trying desperately to calm Madeline and his voice matched the urgency of hers.

But Madeline wouldn't be placated. "She can't do this. She can't make me conduct a piece of commercial claptrap."

"Even if it pays your way to Europe?" The familiar voice at her side was insistent.

Madeline had been so busy glaring at Brew that she hadn't seen Gus join them. She looked up to see Gus Noble's piercing black eyes studying her reaction quite calmly. "There are other ways to earn money, Mr. Noble. This isn't the only scheme in town." In spite of her heated reply, the tone of her voice was even. She didn't want to make a scene and knew that she would have to control her anger—for the moment at least.

"Maybe it's not commercial claptrap. Maybe it's good." Gus was looking down at her, his eyes suddenly filled with a boyish earnestness.

"In that case, Mr. Noble, I would be glad to produce it," she said quietly. "But you have a reputation as a popular songwriter. You are tops in your field, but you are not a classical composer." Madeline was seething under her calm veneer. Working with this man would be impossible!

"Right on both counts, Ms. Mark," Gus concurred easily enough, his strong masculine frame too close to hers. "But this is something different. You're going to like it."

"I don't think so, Mr. Noble. And if I don't like it, the Metropolitan Symphony Orchestra will not produce it. You can be assured of that." Madeline spoke very carefully, each word emphatic. She had made up her mind right then and there to fight the decision if need be. She wouldn't be pushed around, not by Mamie Spencer, certainly not by Gus Noble.

"I don't know about that," Gus said, an inscrutable look in his black eyes. His words were as carefully measured as hers had been. "I'll call on you tomorrow—with the score. You will like it, Ms. Mark, wait and see."

2

Madeline raced up the steps of Jones Hall, her long dark hair flying out behind her in a single ponytail tied with a white ribbon. She hurried down the hall to the symphony offices, looking for Brew Baker. She was determined to let the executive director know exactly how she felt about what had happened the previous evening. Maybe she was being too sensitive. It was true that she was on probation and that her present contract was only for one year. Maybe she should not be so quick to object to the usurpation of her authority, at least not until she had been around longer, and proved herself to the board. But even as she struggled with doubt, Madeline knew she had to object. And it was more than the principle of the thing. Just as she had to take charge of the musicians, she had to establish her authority with the administration. She couldn't buckle under, she just couldn't.

Brew must have been anticipating her arrival, for he was sitting behind his desk doing some paperwork, and his face didn't betray a flicker of surprise when she walked in and slammed the door behind her. "I can't believe you let me walk into that!" Madeline exclaimed. "Why didn't you warn me?"

Brew fidgeted with his red bow tie, obviously flustered. "I'm sorry, Markey," he began. "I tried to warn you. But Mamie Spencer is a powerful woman and she's been on the board for a long time. Still, I never dreamed she had this up her sleeve. It was a surprise to me, too."

"I thought it was your business to know these things." Madeline felt very much on the spot and she knew that she was taking her anger out on the wrong person, but she wanted to make sure that Brew knew how she felt. She knew, too, that she wouldn't be feeling quite so put on the spot if Gus Noble hadn't been there to enjoy her discomfort.

"With Mamie, it isn't always possible to be strictly businesslike." Brew shook his head in exasperation. "She has friends in all the various arts and she's always trying to bring them together. Now that more movies are being made in Houston, I should have known that eventually something to do with film would come home to rest with the symphony."

Madeline looked around the office lined with posters and programs from symphony performances. Brew had been with the orchestra a long time, and everything in the office, from the pictures on the walls to the papers on his desk, demonstrated his love for, and proficiency at, his job. She almost felt sorry for him. It really wasn't his fault. "I didn't mean to sound so harsh," she said softly. "It's just that there's nothing more embarrassing than being trotted out as if you were a trained dog doing tricks. Maybe I wouldn't be so sensitive if I weren't so new around here."

Brew opened a desk drawer, reached for his pipe and began packing it with tobacco. "I know, Markey. And Mamie should be more sensitive to your position. But she means no harm. She has the greatest respect for you. It's just that she sometimes gets carried away with her own enthusiasm. And when you think about it, Mamie's idea isn't so far afield. With the biggest sound stage in the country being built in Houston, it's inevitable that the symphony should begin to do more work of this sort. It's happened in London, in California—this isn't exactly a first. It could be a golden opportunity for us."

"Maybe so," Madeline conceded, "from your point of view. But consider mine. I have a reputation to uphold, and I'm not sure this is to my benefit. Making soundtracks isn't exactly my idea of a worthy endeavor for the conductor of a major symphony." She didn't want to get carried away with her sense of self-importance, but she felt that she had to make her point. "Besides, I've devoted my life to music—it's my first priority. In movies, the music is always secondary."

"Don't be so sure." Brew let out a cloud of fragrant smoke and studied her thoughtfully.

"Remember—Leopold Stokowski did it in *Fantasia*. Look how much that popularized classical music."

Madeline stood up and paced around the room impatiently, her long white smock swirling gracefully above the slim white pants. "That was then and this is now. I'm not Stokowski and Gus Noble isn't exactly Walt Disney."

Brew laughed. "Maybe not, but he stands to do well with this film—he has with others. I've seen most of them and I paid close attention to the soundtracks. Musically, I think you two could work well together. Of course, the final decision is up to you—all musical decisions are yours. But consider the exposure, and as for the money, well—" He broke off into a long, low whistle and rolled his eyes heavenward.

"Money!" Madeline scoffed. "Is that all you have to think about? Suppose the Rolling Stones came in here and wanted us to play backup on their next album?"

Brew pretended to study the posters on the wall. "I'd have to think about it," he said with a laugh. "Somehow I don't think Mick Jagger would have an easy time with Mamie Spencer."

"Well, if it ever comes to that, then count me out." Madeline stopped her pacing and regarded him seriously, tugging at the long black and white scarf she wore around her neck. "I'm working very hard to make this symphony into one of the best in the country. The raw material is all here. I know I can work with this orchestra. And now you want to sell out to some hotshot from Hollywood who's here to make a movie. I don't know, Brew. I just don't know." She didn't mean to sound so angry and she had an urge to sit down and discuss this with him further, but she had a rehearsal.

Brew was watching her closely, and Madeline knew he had something else to say, some last card to play. "Just one thing," he began.

"Yes?" Madeline had reached the doorway and turned to say good-bye.

"This is the way to get the money for the tour—virtually free and clear," Brew reminded her. "The money would be guaranteed, and the board would be happy."

Madeline had known that was coming. Though she knew she had the final say regarding musical decisions, she also knew that Brew was a shrewd business manager and so far even he hadn't been sure that the money could be found in time. Finance was Brew's specialty, and as far as she could tell, he was one of the best. Still, the idea of working with Gus Noble—even for a good cause— made her nervous, and not for purely professional reasons. He had a disturbing effect on her, one she didn't completely understand. That wasn't a good enough reason though, and she knew it.

"Is this the way the board feels?" she asked. She knew Brew would be a good barometer of the board's thoughts and intentions.

Brew hastened to reassure her. "You know they'd never try to push you into anything, Markey, but doing the soundtrack would guarantee the tour, I can promise you that."

"I'll have to think about this, Brew," she said, giving him a smile that indicated she knew what a

difficult position he was in. "Give me some time."
She tugged at her sleeve, looking to see what time it
was. Ten minutes before rehearsal.

"All the time you need," he agreed amiably.
"I'm sure Gus Noble will call you. Listen to him, see
what you think of the music. Don't make a hasty
decision about this, Markey. You might regret it
later. Wait until you talk to Gus. He'll be in touch."

Yes, I just bet he will, Markey thought to herself a
little nervously. He's already been in touch once
and I still don't know what to think of it. He's
destroyed my concentration, he's caught me off
guard—I can't imagine working with him over a
long period of time. Composers are touchy at
best—they always think they know better than the
conductor. All these things raced through her mind
a mile a minute, and finally, when she turned to
face Brew, she was calm again. "I won't regret my
decision, Brew—whatever it is," she assured him.
"We conductors are known for our hasty tempers,
remember?" Her smile bore a trace of her usual
good humor. "But we still have a lot of common
sense."

"Good enough." Brew walked over to the door
and shook her hand. "I'm sorry that Mamie put
you in such an awkward position. That was wrong.
I'll try to keep that from happening again."

"You do that." Madeline shook a finger at him in
mock warning. "And I'll think about this."

"That's all I ask," Brew called after her as she
walked down the hall.

Five minutes. That's all the time I have, Madeline
thought. She made her way through Jones Hall
until she found a seat in the lobby and sat down.

Rehearsal in five minutes. How am I supposed to think about conducting Ravel's *Rhapsodie Espagnole* when somebody wants me to work in film? I have enough on my hands as it is! Now I have to worry about conducting a symphony by someone who's probably just a good songwriter, nothing more. Great, just great.

No, he's more than a songwriter, she reminded herself, thinking back to the moment she'd met him. He's something different. For some reason that thought filled her with alarm. She had been all over the world, had worked with all sorts of different people, but her sixth sense told her that Gus Noble would be trouble—and at a time when she needed it the least.

Worry about that later, she told herself fiercely. Today, this moment, the music is all that matters. Remember the music. It comes first, last and always. She tried to focus on the piece they were scheduled to begin rehearsing that morning. Madeline had spent weeks going over the scores of the works she had chosen for the new season, trying to prepare herself physically and mentally for the difficult task ahead. She simply could not afford to be thrown off her stride.

She leaned back and closed her eyes, willing herself back to the present. She thought of the scores tucked in her attaché case, the notes she knew by heart. Slowly, she calmed herself, reaching deep within to tap her inner resources. When she could feel the music coursing through her mind, she knew she was ready. She stood up, stretched a bit to get the kinks out and walked toward the stage door. She was ready.

The orchestra was ready too, Madeline thought, for they straightened up and eyed her with respect the moment she walked on stage. They looked eager and expectant and ready to get to work. It was always a crucial moment, Madeline knew, starting a new season, and she felt strongly about beginning it the right way. She walked to her place in front of the orchestra, pulled out the score and settled it on the stand in front of her and reached for her baton, removing it from the case she always carried.

"We begin the season with Ravel's *Rhapsodie Espagnole*," she announced calmly. "I know you've all been studying it independently, but it's time we brought all our musical knowledge and talent together. Let us begin."

She raised her baton, signaling the downbeat, and the orchestra fell in with her immediately. Oh, there were a few stragglers, of course; Maurice Spender, for one, and she gave him a quick critical look as he came in late. But for the most part, they were all ready.

As the music flowed from the orchestra, Madeline was filled with the sense of the beauty and power of her work. To bring all these wonderful musicians' talents to bear on the compositions of her choosing was an awesome responsibility and she never took it lightly. She played the orchestra as if it were her own instrument, bending to her work with concentration, her whole body moving with the music, her every gesture conveying some nuance of the piece.

This was a moment of discovery for her. It let her

see how the orchestra thought of the music and showed her the weak spots she would have to single out for special attention. "Do it until you get it right" had always been her motto, and it looked like the Ravel wasn't going to take as much work as she had thought.

This was a surprise to her, for the opening of the piece was a difficult mosaic of tiny motifs for violins and violas. Figaro had really worked on this one, she thought, noticing the way his eyebrows moved up and down as he played with his whole heart. The odd phrasing didn't seem to throw him off for an instant. After a brief pause the second movement, the Malaguena, began. That English horn needs some work, Madeline thought, making a mental note. The fading close of the movement was not quite perfect, but then she hadn't expected it to be—not yet. Before she was through, it would be.

The final movement, a musical representation of a Spanish festival, was absolutely sparkling, and when the run-through was over, Madeline was pleased. She made some notes on her score, indicating the parts she thought needed work, talked briefly about it to the members of the orchestra, then gave them a fifteen-minute break.

She left the stage, going down the side steps and taking a seat down front, and began looking over the score again. A little here, a little there, she thought, this will be lovely. A few musicians asked questions, but for the most part they respected her privacy. Some of them had gone down the hall for coffee, and others were smoking, relishing the moment of relaxation. Madeline knew that this time was important to them too—she knew that they were thinking about how well or how badly they had played. Truth would tell when they went through it for the second time. Do it until you get it right, she reminded herself.

She was about to head for the stage again when she heard a side door open. She looked around, half expecting to see Brew, who often stopped in for part of rehearsals; but when she saw Gus Noble, she wasn't even surprised. Somehow he seemed to her like a man who would barge in without notice. But, in spite of herself, she felt her heart beat faster and a flush rise to her cheeks. Damn him! What kind of power did he hold over her? What was it that caused her to melt at his feet? She was about to ask him to leave, but decided that there was no sense in waving a red flag.

"Good afternoon," she said calmly, praying that her voice wouldn't reveal her emotional turbulence. "I've been expecting to hear from you." But not now, not here, she thought. He looked unusually appealing in a pair of pale blue pinstriped slacks and a white turtleneck cotton shirt. His bold good looks seemed to have no need of the formal attire he had favored the night before. If anything, the casual dress enhanced his lean, muscular frame and athletic build.

"Looks like this is a bad time to talk," he said brusquely, gesturing toward the stage, where some of the musicians were beginning to return to their seats. He had a sheaf of music paper under his arm.

"Yes, it is," Madeline answered quite honestly. "We're just about to do a second run-through, and

I'm afraid I'm going to be here for a while." With one part of her mind, she was reacting to him normally. With another part, she was spontaneously seeing him as a very attractive man. Nothing could disguise his power and energy, and even the horn-rimmed glasses couldn't hide the light of challenge in his black eyes.

"That's all right," he said, taking a seat and looking up at her with a grin. "I'll wait." He settled back comfortably, seemingly oblivious to her coolness. "If I had a program and some popcorn," he laughed, "I'd be perfectly happy." He looked right at home.

Madeline felt a momentary sense of panic—surely he didn't intend to sit there through the rest of the rehearsal! Who did he think he was! Madeline had a second impulse to order him to leave, but it didn't seem worth it. Since he was here, he might as well learn a lesson about real music. Besides, it always added a little fire to the orchestra's performance to have an audience, though a second run-through was early.

She gathered up her score. "Enjoy your front-row seat," she said dryly. "This will be the only one that's free. No popcorn." She turned and walked away, back up on stage. She'd show him what music should be!

When she took her place in front of the musicians, she was the picture of authority. Tapping on the podium to bring them to attention, she lifted her baton, and they plunged in—no stragglers this time. There was even a different expression on the faces of the musicians, as if they were ready to show her that they could do better. And she wanted to do better too. She wanted to show Gus Noble that this was serious music, real music, something perhaps that he could never understand.

The performance was outstanding, almost flawless. If she hadn't known it herself, she would have sworn they were further along than a mere second run-through. Her conducting was infused with passion and energy, and the musicians—every last one of them—responded to it with all their talent and enthusiasm. There was fire and magic in the piece now, where before there had only been technical expertise. What had been craft was now art.

When the piece came to its conclusion, she was surprised to hear the sound of applause coming from behind her. She had been so moved by the orchestra's performance that she had virtually forgotten about Gus sitting there, watching. He had risen to his feet and was applauding enthusiastically. "Bravo! Bravo!" he called out. The musicians all smiled.

At least he's got the language down pat, Madeline thought. And he certainly knows how to draw attention to himself. She was angry that he was making such a spectacle of himself, but looking around, she realized that the members of the orchestra were actually basking in the applause. If this is what it's going to be like working with him, she thought, I can't do it. The man has the most tremendous ego I've ever seen. I don't care how wonderful the track for *Forbidden Stars* is—it simply can't be worth it. There's more than one way to finance a European tour. Still, some part of her was pleased that he appreciated what he had heard and seen. Maybe he wasn't all bad. But then again, maybe he was putting on a show for her benefit.

After she had given a few individual comments to some of the musicians, she dismissed them for the day, and looked around again. Gus was nowhere to be seen. Maybe he left, she thought, surprised to feel a pang of disappointment. Maybe we scared him off. She gathered up her things and went through to the lobby, thinking that she would go up and see if Brew was around, tell him about the rehearsal. There was Gus, pacing around the lobby, a sheaf of music still under his arm.

"I thought you'd gone," she said matter-of-factly.

"Not a chance," he assured her. "I didn't want to be in the way, so I left. I'm sorry if my applauding disrupted anything, but I just couldn't help myself."

So, he has some taste, Madeline thought to herself. "They did rather well today," she said in a satisfied voice.

"Oh, for a second run-through, it was fabulous," Gus assured her. "But that English horn in the second movement needs work, don't you think?"

"Maybe a little," Madeline said a bit defensively, but then she stopped in her tracks. He really did know something about music! "I've already talked to him about it."

"And Figaro McPhee," Gus went on, "is absolutely wonderful. Everything I've ever heard about him is true. He has spirit, he has style, he's just what I want!"

Madeline felt herself being carried along on his

tide of enthusiasm. "And Emily Jane was at her best today, too—the strings were really outstanding." Still, some part of her was holding back. Why didn't he say something about her conducting? "I was very pleased."

"And so you should be." Gus took off his glasses and regarded her seriously. "You brought them all together. I've always thought there should be more women conductors." Gus paused, looked at her, then let out a nervous laugh. "I guess you hear that all the time."

"Right. All the time." Madeline knew that they were dancing around the business they had to do together. Then too, she was becoming increasingly uncomfortable under his perceptive gaze. There was more to this man than met the eye, but she wasn't yet ready to believe the best of him. All right, so he knew something about music. That still didn't make his project the right one for her. She was going to have to be very, very careful.

"So," Gus continued, looking at his watch. "If we hurry, we'll have time for dinner before we start talking music."

"Dinner!" He acted as if it were all prearranged. Madeline had been looking forward to relaxing this evening, and she didn't like being taken for granted.

"Right—hot dogs and a movie. It's all planned." Then, as if he sensed her reluctance, he became persuasive. "Look, I know it's short notice but we could do two things at once—eat and talk about the music. I know you're very busy, but I do think the sooner we talk about this, the sooner we'll know where we stand." He paused and looked at her quizzically, giving her the option. There was a boyish urgency about his appeal.

"All right, dinner," Madeline agreed. "Might as well get it over with." She knew she was being rude, but she couldn't completely shake the feeling that Gus was pushing her.

"It won't be that bad," he said ruefully. "You might even enjoy it. Just because I'm from California and making a movie here, doesn't mean I'm totally stupid or without taste. Give me a chance."

"You're right," she relented, charmed by his forthrightness. There was something irresistible about this man. "I'll give you a chance. Just remember, this is a chance—not a promise."

"I won't forget, as long as you don't forget I told you so." He grinned impetuously. He was leading her to the door of the elevator to the parking garage. "Let's take my car."

"Fine, fine." Madeline would have agreed with anything just to get the show on the road at that point. "Let's go."

He talked nonstop all the way down in the elevator and through the parking garage, and Madeline couldn't help but be impressed by his wit and intelligence. Maybe she'd underestimated him. Maybe there really was something here. Only time would tell.

When he led her to the door of the red Checker cab parked in the parking lot, Madeline had to laugh. She remembered it from the night before. Like everything else about Gus Noble, it was eye-catching and flashy. "Here you go, Ms. Mark," he said with a flourish, opening her door.

Madeline got in, reached over to unlock the door

on the driver's side and waited until he had settled in to speak. "Let's get one thing straight, Gus. My friends call me Markey."

"Thanks," he said lightly, his eyes meeting hers directly, a promise in his voice. "I'd like to be your friend." He grinned. "Let's go hear some music, Markey."

3

⚬⚬⚬⚬⚬⚬⚬⚬⚬⚬⚬⚬

Where are you taking me?" Madeline asked after
Gus had been driving for quite a while. He turned
off Main Street and doubled back to Montrose,
parking in front of the Plaza Hotel.

"Be right back," he said mysteriously as he got
out of the car and went inside.

Madeline thought longingly of her own condominium only a few blocks away. I could walk it, she
thought with sudden determination. I could be
home in fifteen minutes. But she knew that would
only postpone the inevitable. If she didn't talk to
Gus now, she'd just have to do it another time.
Fifteen minutes ticked by, and she began to grow
impatient. She was just about to get out of the car
and start looking for Gus when he came racing
through the hotel doors, carrying a wicker basket.

"What's that?" Madeline asked, eyeing it suspiciously as he got in beside her. "Don't tell me you have some weird pet you always travel with."

"That," Gus said with no small satisfaction, "is for our dinner."

"A picnic?" Madeline was enchanted by the prospect, but she didn't want him to know it. He was certainly going to a lot of trouble to impress her.

"A working picnic," Gus corrected her, a knowing grin on his face. "Besides, I don't know any good restaurants in Houston yet. But I will. Bear with me this one time and I'll make it all up to you later."

Madeline laughed. He was charming—even if he was used to getting his own way. "Okay," she said, "but you owe me a dinner—remember that." She knew she was flirting with the future, implying that she'd see him again, and she was astonished at her own lack of caution.

Gus seemed to read her thoughts. He grinned. "If that means you'll go out with me again, you can be sure I won't forget it," he promised. "You can pick the restaurant."

He was heading toward the freeway now, and Madeline wondered about his destination. "If you're planning on having a picnic, are you sure you know where you're going? We just passed up the prettiest park in Houston back by the hotel."

"We're not going to a park," Gus said. "We're going somewhere else."

He didn't seem lost, so Madeline settled back to enjoy the ride, curious to see what would happen next. He must have had something in mind even if he didn't want to tell her what it was. He seemed like a man with definite plans. As a matter of fact, she wouldn't have been at all surprised if he'd called from Jones Hall to order the picnic. Gus Noble seemed like a man who knew what he wanted and set out to get it any way he could.

He was full of surprises, she thought, determined not to be caught off guard again. But when he turned into the driveway of the Gulf Winds Drive-In Movie Theater off the freeway, she couldn't believe it. "What's this?" she demanded. She'd never in her whole life been to a drive-in movie. Living all over the world as the sheltered daughter of diplomats certainly had its advantages, she knew, but there were drawbacks too, serious omissions in her experience.

"I said we were going to hear some music—my music," Gus said. "Unfortunately, this is the only place in town where any of the movies I've worked on is playing. It's not the best way to see a movie." Here he seemed genuinely apologetic, but then his voice brightened. "But think about it as an adventure—like you doing the concerts in the park. I'm just showing you my work outdoors."

"An unfortunate comparison," Madeline said a bit dryly. "But I won't argue the point. Still, it's not even dark yet—how long are we going to have to sit here and wait? I don't have all night, you know."

"The time will fly," Gus promised her. "By the time we're through with our picnic dinner, it'll be show time, I promise you."

Inwardly, Madeline fumed a bit. This was time,

precious time to her, and she felt that, in some obscure way, Gus was taking advantage of the situation. Outwardly, he was all charm, but she knew better than to succumb to that. At least she already knew his ulterior motive. She pitied any woman who was foolish enough to fall for this sort of deliberate campaign.

"C'mon," Gus said. He got out of the car and reached into the back seat for the picnic basket. "Let's eat."

"Where?" Madeline looked around. Somehow, she'd just assumed that they'd eat in the car.

Gus gestured toward the screen. "See up there?" There was a picnic table and a small version of a playground with swings and slides. "This is the perfect place for our picnic. Not too many kids yet. And we'll both get some fresh air. If I were at home, I would have brought two lawn chairs and a cooler full of beer and we could have watched the movie outside."

"All right." Madeline felt a bit testy. Enough was enough. She followed him up to the picnic table and began to help as he opened the basket. The Plaza's incredibly elegant china and silver was the first thing to appear, followed by two crystal wine-glasses and cloth napkins. "This looks lovely," she said appreciatively, but her face fell a bit as she looked into the basket. "Where's the food?"

"Oh, the food," Gus said. "I can't believe they forgot that." His expression was one of mock indignation, but when he looked up at her, his face was creased by a wide smile. "I thought we'd get the food here."

"Here?" Madeline looked back toward the refreshment stand with dismay. Not junk food, please, not junk food. It had been a hard day. She didn't want to add indigestion to her list of problems.

"Right! You haven't lived until you've had a chili dog at a drive-in. If the lady will allow me to order for her, I'll be right back with dinner."

"The lady doesn't seem to have much of a choice," Madeline informed him. Besides, her stomach was beginning to growl. It had been a long time since lunch.

Gus trotted off to the refreshment stand and vanished inside. God only knows what he'll come up with, Madeline thought to herself. Still, she had to admit that he was interesting. A little odd, but intriguing. She looked around at the rows and rows of speakers, at the few cars beginning to fill the ranks for the evening show. A couple of kids came up and began to play on one of the swing sets.

The burning summer sun was beginning to set when Gus came back, his arms filled with cardboard cartons. Madeline was admiring the blaze of color in the sky when she saw him standing next to her and grinning. "Dinner is served, Mademoiselle Markey," he announced. "At least I assume it's Mademoiselle."

"You assume correctly," she told him, wondering if there was a Mrs. Gus Noble somewhere in California. No, she told herself, I can't imagine a woman who'd put up with him for any length of time.

Gus began to unload the food—Madeline

thought it all looked revolting. "Let's see here," Gus said. "We've got chili dogs and tacos and nachos and chocolate-covered almonds and Cokes." He stopped to pour a Coke into the crystal wineglass from its paper cup. "What sounds good?"

"To be perfectly honest, not much," she said.

Gus groaned and clutched his chest in mock horror. "Don't tell me you're a food snob, too." He seemed resigned. "Oh, well, I guess it makes sense—music snob, food snob. They seem to go together." He looked her right in the eye. "Markey, Markey, what are you doing? You're going to miss out on all the fun in life!"

"I am not," she shot back. "I'm not a snob. Just give me one of those tacos." Gus reached over and plopped one on the china plate. She decided to go along with all this. Besides, the taco wasn't half-bad. She washed it down with her drink and helped herself to a chili dog.

Who did he think he was, telling her she was a snob, telling her that she was missing out on all the good things in life? She'd lived all over Europe with her family, she'd studied in the best schools, eaten in the finest restaurants. But all along, she'd been insulated and protected by the life in diplomatic circles. Wherever her father had been sent, she'd simply learned to adjust. Her parents had always made sure she had the best of everything. Still, she sometimes had the feeling she'd missed something, something other people had always had and took for granted. Things like hot dogs and drive-in movies.

Gus's voice broke into her thoughts. "Hey, Markey." His voice was soft and caressing. "Don't look so solemn. What are you thinking about?"

"Oh, this," she said with a small smile, gesturing at the cars around them, the children playing on the swings. "I've never done anything like this before."

"See?" Gus reminded her. "I told you it wouldn't be all bad. If you think this is fun, wait until you see the movie." He stopped to think about what she'd said. "You mean to tell me you've never been to a drive-in movie?" His voice evidenced his disbelief.

"Never." Madeline felt as though she were admitting some sort of personal failure. "I don't think they have them in Europe, which is really where I grew up. And later, when I came to New York to go to Juilliard, I never had the time." She saw no reason to add that all her energies had been directed toward her music, as they had been all her life, that she'd simply never had time for anything else, except once when . . . She pushed aside that memory, never letting it surface completely, ignoring the pain.

"Jeez!" Gus sounded as if he couldn't comprehend it. "Have you ever been to a circus?"

"Of course! That's pushing it a little far, Gus," she said with a sigh. "Besides, I'm not here to talk about childhood deprivations. I'm here to talk about work. Remember? If you expect to woo me with hot dogs and Cokes, you've got another think coming."

"I'm not trying to woo you with anything," he said smoothly. "I don't need to. The music will do that for me." He had no doubts whatsoever about his talent, that was clear.

"Then why aren't you telling me about it?" Madeline reminded herself of the time she was wasting. If she wasn't careful, Gus Noble was going to charm her into doing whatever he wanted. The man was positively dangerous.

"I don't have to. You'll see for yourself when the movie starts. This isn't my very best work—the music for *Forbidden Stars* is, I know that. But this will give you an indication of how far I've come. And I don't think I had very far to go. If you don't like the music, if you're not intrigued by it, then I'll know we can't work together."

"Fair enough." Night was beginning to fall around them and Madeline wondered when the film would begin. Sure enough, she could see lights beginning to appear on the screen with the theater's commercial for the refreshment stand, and then some previews of coming attractions. "Hadn't we better get back to the car?"

"Right." Gus gathered up the trash and disposed of it neatly while she repacked the basket with the china and crystal. Coming back, he held out the remaining Coke to her and she took it. "Save this—we'll share it later with popcorn."

As they walked back to the car through the darkness settling around them, Madeline felt increasingly nervous. There was something about Gus that touched her deeply, and as much as she hated to admit it, she was curious to hear about his music. Settling into the front seat on the passenger side, she noticed that the large front seat gave her a lot of space. She was glad he didn't drive a sports car.

"All right, tell me about this movie," she said as the previews began to fade away, and she sensed that it was about to begin.

"I don't need to tell you anything," he returned confidently. He rolled up the window so he could attach the speaker and then he adjusted the volume to his satisfaction. "Watch the movie and listen to the music."

"All right." Madeline hadn't expected such a matter-of-fact reaction. Somehow, she'd imagined that he'd want to go on at length, talking about his work. Well, she'd see if it was worth talking about.

She settled back in her seat and waited for the film to start, sipping at the cold drink. She didn't have time to go to movies often, and she didn't much think she'd like this one—*Prince of the Rodeo* was the title—and she could imagine the dreadful country music that would go along with it. She was surprised that Gus would dare to bring her to see it. Surely he would know that it gave a bad impression.

She looked over at him in the darkness and the light glinted off his glasses as he gave her a brilliant smile. "Just wait," he said. "I think you'll like the music. Maybe not the story, but the music. Just wait."

She gave a sigh and settled back, expecting the worst. But when the movie began, she was surprised. The scene on the screen in front of them was of a corral filled with wild horses, animals in terror, all rushing around and crashing into each other. As unlikely as it seemed, the music captured their beauty and their fear in equal measure. Somehow Gus had caught it—it wasn't classical music, but it wasn't country either—it was something very different and very special. She sat up and watched with interest, listening for more of the story.

As the movie unfolded, she saw that *Prince of the Rodeo* was about Joe Carver, a horse rancher who had always wanted to be a rodeo cowboy, but he had put his dreams aside to struggle with the ranch to support his family. The beginning of the movie was filled with action and color—wonderful scenes of ranching and rodeos, and Madeline soon found that she was completely enthralled, both with the story and the music. By this time, Joe Carver was beginning to show a profit on his ranch. He chose a wild horse and began to tame it, always with the idea of making it big on the rodeo circuit.

Madeline looked over and saw that Gus was stretching uncomfortably. He seemed nervous about her reaction, despite all his brash assertions of confidence.

"You look uncomfortable behind that steering wheel," she suggested impulsively. "Why don't you move over a bit? There's plenty of room."

"Thanks," he said, and suited the action to the word. He moved over to the middle of the seat and stretched his long legs gratefully, moving his arms along the back of the seat.

Madeline almost immediately regretted her generosity, for she was soon aware of every move he made, every breath he took. "Are you sure I can't get you some popcorn?" he whispered.

"Sure, sure, if you want," Madeline whispered back. "Now go on. I'm trying to listen."

He gave a satisfied smile and let himself out of the car. Madeline missed the warmth of his body next to her, but she was soon swept up again in the story and the music unfolding in front of her, and when Gus let himself back into the car, she shushed him almost immediately. He turned up the volume on the speaker.

They sat there, sharing the popcorn, and Madeline leaned forward once or twice to catch a phrase or a bit of music, regretting even the small distraction of the noise of the popcorn. The music really was wonderful, she thought, and when she brushed Gus's hand in the popcorn box, she drew back quickly and instinctively. She was beginning to feel too close to him, she thought. The music was simply too revealing.

There were long lyrical sections when Joe was taming his horse, Sunrise. The scene contained little dialogue but the music was a perfect representation of their emotional states at the moment—the horse's incredible fear of the man approaching with the bridle, and the man's desperate need to tame the horse, to make him his own. The music carried the story, and Madeline found that she was eager to hear more. As she'd expected, the music did have overtones of country guitars during the rodeo scenes, but they were special too, as if Gus had taken the simple form and given it new life and dignity. Times had changed for Joe, and the rodeo wasn't what he had imagined. When he achieved his success, he discovered that he really wanted to be back on the ranch with his wife and children, who had been glad to see him finally satisfy his dream.

Maybe she was a snob, Madeline reflected seriously, maybe she had tunnel vision. Madeline knew she was in the presence of real talent. Granted, the kind of music he wrote was different from the kind she usually liked, but it was real music, powerful and soul searing. She'd underestimated him, and she felt momentarily embarrassed. Everything she saw, everything she heard, made her want to know him better. She could feel his arm stretched out on the seat behind her and she wanted to lean back against it, wanted to nestle into the man's shoulder just as she wanted to drown in the man's music. She could work with this sort of talent, she definitely could. She would do it even if she didn't need the money for a European tour. It would be a privilege.

When the movie was ending and Joe Carver returned to his ranch and his life before the rodeo, the air was filled with a haunting theme of home—music so filled with longing and love that Madeline could feel it touch her heart. The music continued to play as the credits rolled.

When she heard the cars around them starting up and lights began to flash, Madeline felt as if she were being jolted sharply back to reality. She sat there in silence for a few minutes, sorry that it was over, wishing that she could see it again, and wondering what she could possibly say to Gus, who was looking at her expectantly. He pulled his glasses slowly down the length of his nose, then reached out and set them on the windshield. For a fleeting instant, she thought that he was going to kiss her. She almost wished he would. But he only stretched and moved back behind the steering wheel, putting the key in the ignition.

"Don't go yet," she said, startled by the sound of her own voice in the silence of the car. "We'd just have to wait in line behind all those other cars."

"All right," Gus agreed, putting his glasses on again. "We can talk just as well right now. What do you think?"

"I think I like it," she said honestly. "It's not what I expected, but I'm very impressed." Suddenly she didn't want to play games with this man anymore. He had talent, and she wanted to recognize it. It was her professional responsibility.

"I thought you would be," he said, and there was a trace of the self-confidence she had noticed in him from the beginning. "You're good at what you do—I'd expect you to like it. I'm good at what I do, too. Besides, our work really isn't so very far apart, you know."

"How's that?" She wanted to hear more. Now she was definitely interested.

"A conductor takes a great piece of music and interprets it, looks it over, sees it in his or her own special way, then makes the orchestra see it the same way. What I do is take a story and translate it into music—it's another language, from words to song. Surely you can see that."

"Oh, I do," Madeline assured him. "I guess I

never saw any movies where the music was as interesting and as important as the story."

"Well, it isn't in all of them," Gus admitted. "I was lucky to work with the director of *Prince of the Rodeo*. But I knew that the soundtrack was equally as important to him as the acting or the script. I don't work with people who think music is an afterthought. If it's not as important to them as it is to me, then I don't want to bother with it. I'm too good to waste my time and my energy that way."

She couldn't help but be a little bit irritated by Gus's sense of his own self-worth. Then again, she reminded herself that if he hadn't had it in the first place, he might never have made it in the music business or in the movies. They were cutthroat worlds, both of them, and you had to be tough to be a success. She knew that. She'd had to be tough to get where she was.

"What about *Forbidden Stars?*" she asked. "Are the director and the producer as interested in music as the people who did this movie were?"

"I guess so." Gus gave a short laugh. "They're the same people. They've got a good story and they want some good music. Granted, it's a change from a story like this to a science fiction movie, but they do quality work. And that's where you come in."

"Me?" Madeline was surprised to find that she was taking it for granted that she would work with him.

"Sure. You're the best at what you do, too." He leaned forward and gave her a penetrating gaze. "And you know it. I've seen you conduct—and not just at the Fourth of July symphony performance. I saw you at Wolf Trap when you were conducting works by American composers with the Boston Philharmonic. You're magic. You know how to make music better. That's why I want to work with you. When I found out that *Forbidden Stars* was being shot in Houston, I thought this was the perfect opportunity to work with you. You're my first and only choice."

He was so intense that Madeline felt a momentary urge to retreat back into her shell. She needed to keep her distance. She was learning too much too fast and loving every minute of it. She'd have to keep a firm rein on her emotions.

"Well, we'll see," she said a bit primly, reluctant to commit herself solely on the basis of what she'd heard that evening. "You've been carrying that score around with you all day—what are you waiting for?"

Gus flipped on the overhead light, reached in the back seat for the score and tossed it in her direction. "Sure. Take a look. See what you think."

Madeline looked over the first few pages with interest, imagining a living, breathing music from the black and white notes in front of her. She could hear it inside her head, and she liked what she heard. She began to look through the pages more and more quickly, but Gus reached out for them and tossed them in the back seat again.

"Wait! I was just getting a feel for what you're doing!" She desperately wanted to look at it some more.

"I know a better way," Gus said, turning on the

engine and heading for the exit. "I'm going to play it for you. Tonight. Right now. You'll love it."

She probably would, Madeline thought. She resolved to be patient. She'd already learned one thing from Gus Noble—not to underestimate him. That was one mistake she wouldn't make again.

4

How on earth did you get the Plaza Hotel to put a grand piano in your room?" Madeline was flabbergasted.

Gus grinned. "It wasn't easy. Let's just say I had to pull a few strings and pay them an arm and a leg. After that, it was easy." He shut the door behind them, walked over to the couch and turned on the lamps, giving the room more light.

Madeline looked around the suite of rooms where Gus was living during his stay in Houston. There was nothing fancy about it, nothing that would indicate one of the most successful songwriters in the country was living there. Nothing, that is, except the grand piano next to the windows overlooking the street. She had to admit to herself that this man had a certain inimitable style. Dropping her purse on the couch, she walked over to the piano, sat down and ran her fingers across the keyboard. "It's even in tune," she said, looking up at Gus.

"But of course," he confirmed. "What would I do with a piano that's out of tune?" He sat down on the piano bench next to her and started playing chopsticks. It was an open invitation.

"I can do that, too," Madeline retorted with a smile, falling in with him easily, knowing that had been the pattern of the evening. It worried her a little, since she was used to setting her own pace and those of others. But it seemed the thing she did naturally with him. Maybe they would work well together. Maybe they would make good partners. She looked over at him surreptitiously through her long black lashes. His rugged male profile was deep in concentration, and once again, she realized how handsome he was.

As if sensing her glance, Gus turned his head slightly in her direction, never missing a beat on the piano, and gave her a slow wink. Their shoulders were touching and the music they played together was in complete harmony. Almost as if he wanted to test her further, Gus increased the tempo, going faster and faster. Madeline had no trouble keeping up with him, and for a few moments both were completely engrossed in their fingers on the keyboard. Then, when they had been through each stanza three times, playing so fast neither one could play any faster, they broke into laughter, simultaneously defeated by their own game.

Gus put his arm around her shoulder, their heads touching as they laughed. "You're okay, Markey," he said in between laughs.

"Thanks a lot," Madeline said. "I'm glad I have your approval." They were both laughing more than the situation warranted, and both seemed to sense it. Somehow, the ice had finally been broken.

Gus stopped, a new look on his face. His black eyes met hers, probing for something more. "Approval is something of an understatement. You know that by now, don't you?"

Somehow she did know that, but she was afraid of it, terrified of where it might lead. She had to put a stop to this before it went any further. They had work to do and she had no intention of being sidetracked. "It's late, Gus," she said, sliding down the piano bench, moving away. "And I'm here on business."

Gus withdrew his arm as if she had slapped him. "That's right, you are," he said, staging his own retreat. "I almost forgot. For a moment there, I thought you were a real live woman. I won't make the same mistake twice—you're a musician, first, last and always." Angrily, he got up from the piano and headed toward the small kitchenette off to one side of the living room. "I think I'll have a glass of wine. Will you join me, Ms. Mark?" His voice was formal and distant.

"Gus—" she started, then, knowing it was pointless, said mechanically, "Yes, thank you. That would be nice." She had hurt him, she knew that. And she was sorry, but there was nothing she could say to make it all right. Her heart twisted in pain as she turned toward the window and looked pensively out at the night. She could see Butera's Delicatessen and, down the street, the Glassell School of Art and the Museum of Fine Arts. All the world seemed paired off in couples, some eating a late supper at Butera's, others headed for Zimm's Wine Bar or Caprice, the Plaza's nightclub. They walked hand in hand or had their arms locked around each other, lovers all. One couple sitting in front of Butera's raised their glasses in a toast, and Madeline felt a pang of jealousy. She had never known that kind of sharing. Her work had always come first.

That's what made her attraction to Gus Noble so terrifying. She knew what it was like to respond to a man in this way and it frightened her to think that it might be happening again. During her second year at Boston, she'd fallen madly in love with the visiting conductor Martin Singer. It had been an unsuitable pairing, she knew that now, but at the time it had seemed as inevitable as the change of seasons.

The minute Martin had walked into the rehearsal hall, she had fallen under his spell. With his lionlike mane of black hair streaked with gray, he'd been an imposing presence in her life from the first moment. When he'd taken her under his wing for private instruction, she hadn't been able to believe her luck. Their mutual interest had sparked into love, and Markey had given her whole heart, fighting the certain knowledge that their affair had no future. Martin was much too old for her, forty-five to her twenty-eight, and he had just divorced his third wife. When he left after six months, her heart had been broken, and the entire orchestra had seemed to sense it. For an entire year, she'd had to struggle to regain her professional balance, fighting depression that even threatened her physical health.

Then one day the cloud was gone and Markey realized she was over him. The work that had been her solace became her abiding passion, the only thing she could trust. Since that terrible year, she'd kept herself free of possible romantic entanglements. Oh, she'd had dates, which she privately thought of as "escorts," but they were simply friends, nothing more. Sometimes she regretted her fate, wondering if she had let life pass her by. Maybe she was too old, maybe . . .

Gus returned to the living room with two glasses of white wine. His manner was subdued and he didn't look Madeline in the eye until he handed her a drink. "I'm sorry," he said simply, and he was obviously sincere. "I apologize, Markey. I shouldn't have lost my temper. That was uncalled for. You are here on business, business that's important to me, too."

Madeline had her regrets as well. "No, don't apologize. I deserved it. I was being high-handed." She smiled weakly. "An occupational hazard, I'm afraid." Their eyes met with an electric thrill, and Madeline again realized the intensity of her emotions. This man was more important to her than she dared to admit.

"What do you say we start over again?" Gus said, suddenly taking back the wineglass he had just handed her. "I've got a great idea!" he said with exuberance.

"Okay, but—" Madeline didn't have a chance to finish.

"No buts allowed," Gus said with an irrepressible grin. He put both their glasses on the piano. "We're going to get off on the right foot yet, if it takes me all night. Come on." Taking her by the hand, he led her to the door and back out into the hotel corridor.

"You aren't kidding, are you?" Madeline couldn't help but giggle at his playfulness. They were standing outside his door, just as they had earlier.

"Never," Gus assured her solemnly. "I'm a man of my word. You'll know that about me soon enough." And with that, he flung open the door dramatically. "My home sweet home," he said with a flourish of his hand, welcoming her again.

"Oh, this is lovely." Falling into the spirit of things, Madeline pretended to have just arrived. "My oh my—a piano. How did you ever get the Plaza—"

"Okay," Gus said, rolling his eyes and shrugging, as if he were beginning to feel a little silly. "That's far enough. We've been there before." He put both his hands on her shoulders and said earnestly, "Why don't we get down to business?"

"I couldn't have said it better myself," Madeline replied, grateful for his high spirits. He had saved the evening. "I was beginning to think you were stalling or getting cold feet." She couldn't resist teasing him. "Are you sure you've really written a symphony?" Even after all the kidding around, the delays, she was curious. He had been baiting her all evening, leading her on with one thing or another. She had taken the bait. She was hooked.

"There's not much else I'm more sure of in this

world," Gus said, sitting down at the piano. He started playing a sweet, lilting melody with one hand. With the other, he reached up for a sheaf of papers and placed them on the stand, turning the pages until he found what he wanted. He smiled up at her as he began playing in earnest now.

Madeline stood next to the piano, listening, watching his long, slender fingers move gracefully up and down the black and white keyboard. He was good, she had to admit, better than most, and she found herself being lulled into a pleasant, untroubled mood where time seemed to reach out into a quiet infinity. His fingers were sure, strong and capable. The music filled the room as passionately as moonlight filled the darkness. There was something sensual about his hands touching the ivory keys, something exciting, something erotic. She tried to dismiss such thoughts, but it was hard for her to separate his touch from the music that enveloped her, held her captive.

Madeline picked up her glass of wine and took a sip, smiling at him. "Nice," she whispered, and they both knew she was talking about the music, not the wine. Gus watched her face with a dreamy quality in his eyes as the music swelled and grew under his touch, a wild wind moving about restlessly. He had shifted into another gear, moved them into another world with his fingertips as surely as if he had transplanted them physically. It was a world they shared, one they both knew by heart. Wordlessly, they spoke the same language.

Gus knew what he was doing, and in a few minutes, the music had changed from the lovely lilting melody to a pressured, harsh tempo—very contemporary, very new. Madeline felt her heart begin to soar. There was power in this, and she found herself reacting time after time to the dramatic swings in mood. Putting her glass back down, she leaned unselfconsciously with both elbows on the shiny surface. Her long ponytail fell over one shoulder and the silken black hair against the clear porcelain of her skin was a contrast as classic as that of the keyboard. She was so caught up in the music that she was oblivious to her own radiant reflection in the highly polished wood. This was different. This was unexpected. This was genius. She recognized it at once.

"What's the story?" she finally asked. She wanted to know everything there was about this music.

Softly, Gus began to speak, his eyes moving back and forth from her face to the keyboard, his voice as magical as the music. "It takes place in some distant point in the future. Everything's become very compartmentalized and regimented. Everyone lives in tiny, cell-like cubicles, the world being so overpopulated that there's scarcely any elbow room." He stretched his own elbows out to make a point, the music billowing, flowing.

Entranced, Madeline quietly moved around the piano and sat down beside Gus, afraid she'd miss something if she was too far away. "Go on," she said. "I'm listening."

"Space travel is the prerogative only of government officials and the very rich," Gus continued, his eyes now on the piano. "Everyone else is bound and chained to jobs, routine existences. They do the same things day after day, over and over again. The human spirit is being pulverized, mechanized." The music began to pound harder and harder, a giant buzz-saw, a great hammer. Gus was lost in the music, his dark head bent over the keyboard, his eyes following the difficult patterns his hands had mastered as the composition softened to a complicated and repetitive movement, the only bit of melody a monotone.

Madeline sat beside him, acutely aware of her shoulder brushing against his, of his vitality, his passion. When he looked up again, this time his eyes crinkled around the edges as the mood of the music changed to a triumphant, whimsical note. "For normal guys like the hero of the movie, the stars are just something seen at night, something to dream about."

"Forbidden stars," Madeline interjected. It was all beginning to make sense.

Gus nodded, but didn't stop telling the story. "The hero is a spaceship mechanic and his assigned role in life is doubly hard because he sees the spaceships, knows what they look like on the inside, understands their powerful engines. He knows what they can do, where they can go. He works the night shift at the spaceport and every night he goes home after work and looks up at the stars and thinks about how cruel it is. . . ." Once again, Gus concentrated on the music his fingers were making.

"Like listening to music and never being able to make it." Madeline was talking to herself, her eyes on the score. She wanted to know what the other instruments would be doing, to understand the whole plan.

Gus looked over at her in surprise. "A composer without an orchestra." He didn't stop playing the piano. "How did you know?"

Madeline looked at him, her gray eyes full of understanding. "That's my job, remember? Interpretation."

Gus smiled, as much to himself as to her, and returned his energies to the piano for the finale. "He starts studying celestial navigation and wants to escape, to become a space buccaneer. He's good at what he does. He understands spaceships better than almost anyone. He knows how they're made, what parts are important, what can be done without."

Gus seemed to have completely forgotten about her. He might have been talking to himself, playing the piano for himself alone. "The movie ends when he eludes all the officials and steals a spaceship to go off and find the forbidden stars." The music rose to a crescendo, the lovely and lilting star theme he had played at the beginning, reaching a climax in a sudden burst of energy.

When he had finished, they were both silent for a moment, his fingers still on the keyboard. Madeline was the first to speak, softly so as not to break the spell. "You've done it, Gus," she whispered, reaching out for his hand. "You've made the spaceship. It's going to fly. It really is." She looked up at his black eyes and saw the fire in them and knew they reflected that of her own. She looked at him with new respect, new admiration. He'd been right. She was wrong.

"That's what I hoped you'd say," was his husky reply, and when he bent to brush his lips against hers, she wasn't surprised. They had both known it was coming. It had been inevitable. There was nothing she could do to stop it, nothing she wanted to do. Their hearts and minds were one at that moment, and Madeline gave herself up to the passion that moved within her, not knowing for sure whether it was for the music or the man. Maybe there wasn't a difference. Right now, it didn't matter.

As his lips touched hers, she placed one hand on his cheek, her fingers searching out the strong line of his jaw. The kiss was deep and strong, and the fire that had been waiting to be lit was ignited. His arm went around her slender waist, pulling her close, his tongue insisting on its own way. They both surrendered to the moment, neither seeming to want to break away.

When finally, reluctantly, Gus drew back, his eyes were fond and loving. "Thanks, Markey. Thanks a lot." He ran a slow finger across her lips.

"You're welcome," was Madeline's almost formal answer, a thrill of pleasure racing through her. Her eyes locked with his and she was ignoring the warnings of caution at the back of her thoughts. She looked down at her hand in his, and knew at that moment, all warnings aside, she had met a man she could lose her heart to.

As if he sensed her slight withdrawal and understood that she needed some time, Gus moved away from the personal question that lay unspoken between them to a professional one. "Does that mean you'll do it?" He was almost bashful about asking the question.

Madeline squeezed his hand, maybe a reassurance that they'd get back to the personal, maybe a thank you for understanding. In any case, she pounced on the question—the answer was ready. "You bet," she said with a grin. "When do we start?"

Gus ran his fingers across the keyboard, moving from one end to the other, a musical crash that gave vent to his excitement. "How about yesterday afternoon?" He reached for the sheaf of papers and, taking her by the hand, moved over to the couch.

They worked together on the score, Gus sitting on the couch, explaining, Madeline sitting cross-legged on the floor, her elbows propped up on the coffee table. Their excitement was high. Madeline had never been more enthusiastic and the animated flush on her face made her even more beautiful. She asked questions and made suggestions late into the night. Gus listened intently, argued occasionally, and kept their glasses filled with wine.

"It's very special," Madeline finally said. It was late, early morning actually. The wine was gone, the music exhausted. For the first time in hours, she was suddenly self-conscious, all too aware of Gus's presence across from her, so close she could reach out and touch him.

His black eyes met hers, the unspoken question reasserting itself. It had been there all along. He reached out his hand, touched her soft black hair, pushed back a stray tendril. "Yes, it is very special."

They sat there for a long moment, their eyes locked in silent torment. Afraid of what she saw, Madeline closed her eyes, turned her head slightly and kissed his hand. When she opened her eyes again, the answer was clear. She would not back away again. She knew she had offered more than just her heart. She waited expectantly as Gus leaned forward to brush her lips with his, and as the pressure became more insistent, she gave in to it, welcomed it. It was as if all the tension of the evening, the excitement of the music, had drained away and left them with what had been between them from the very beginning. They were too aware of their desire for each other to continue long without acknowledging it. Madeline knew that as certainly as she knew that she should find some way to fight her feelings.

"Gus, Gus," she breathed, caught in his arms. "We shouldn't be doing this. It will make everything so much harder." But she knew as she spoke the words that she couldn't convince him to stop. She didn't want him to stop.

"We are doing this," he said a bit gruffly, looking down at her with desire. "We have been for hours." He held out his hand to her, pulled her up on the couch beside him. "We can't stop now."

There was a strange truth in that, Madeline thought to herself as she curled up beside him, waiting, anticipating the next kiss. The music had been an intimate bond all evening, she thought as she parted her lips for his tongue. It had been from the very beginning. She gave herself to the kiss with new fervor, holding nothing back, and when Gus's fingers found the buttons of her smock and sought the soft flesh above her breasts, she made no protest, returning the gesture, reaching for the buttons of his shirt. As his mouth trailed fiery kisses along the line of her throat down to the delicate flesh of her breasts, she cried with pleasure, running her fingers through his hair, all caution forgotten.

Gus continued his exploration, unbuttoning her smock all the way and opening the front fastening of her bra to let her breasts fall free for his touch. All the while, he was gently rearranging their bodies, until they were lying side by side on the comfortable sofa. He kissed every inch of her breasts, lingering over the taut pink nipples lovingly, teasing them slowly with his tongue until Madeline thought she could stand it no longer. She tugged at his hair until he lifted his face to gaze at her quizzically. "What is it?"

"I don't know," she said softly. "I just felt so wonderful that I wanted you to stop. I wanted you to start over." Then, as if she were startled by her own admission of her feelings, she said lightly, "This is really adolescent, isn't it?"

"A bit." Gus nodded and looked down at her affectionately, his slender fingers ruffling her long black hair, teasing her. "But I wanted you to have a choice. I didn't want to say let's go to bed—I didn't want to scare you. I wanted to take it slow and easy, and then you decide for yourself what you want."

Madeline laughed mischievously. "How does a songwriter know so much about female psychology?"

"I don't," Gus admitted, looking her right in the eye. "Somehow, there's something about you that lets me know what's right for you—for us. You've been watching me all night. I've been watching you, too."

"And?" Madeline's voice was soft—soft and sensual. She waited to see what he would say next.

"We belong together. It's as simple as that." Gus kissed the back of her neck, his face nuzzled in her long, soft hair.

"For now, at least," Madeline agreed, pushing aside all her doubts, all her fears. "Let's not think any further ahead than now, this very moment. It may be all we have." She stood up and walked to the bedroom door, turned and looked to see the expression on his face. "Coming?" she asked gently. "I might change my mind," she teased.

"Oh, no you won't," Gus said, coming to her side. "I'm not going to give you a chance." He swooped down and picked her up in his arms, carrying her across the room to the king-sized bed, placing her gently upon its length. He let her watch him as he walked around the room, switching on the bedside light, turning off the overhead light.

"Now," he said softly as he stretched out beside her, "you have me completely in your power." He leaned forward and teased her lips with tiny feather kisses. "I'll do exactly what you tell me."

Madeline laughed a low, husky, sensual laugh, teasing his ear with her tongue. "I don't think I have to tell you what to do."

He only nodded, burying his face in her soft white shoulder, pulling off her silk smock with his free hand. She sat up and reached for his shirt, returning the gesture. Gus pulled her close, kissing her passionately, then gently pushed her away. "You are so lovely," he said, looking down at her breasts, then up into her eyes. "You are the loveliest woman I've ever seen."

"And you," Madeline assured him, her finger teasing the tangle of hair on his chest, "are the most beautiful man I've ever seen."

It all seemed too easy, too natural, and Madeline was always suspicious when things seemed too right. When Gus leaned down to cover her mouth with his own and reached for the zipper of her slacks, she felt a momentary impulse to stop him—to tell him anything, that it was too soon, that she didn't want this, not now, not yet; but as Gus's hand slowly stroked the cool flesh of her flat stomach, she knew that it was no use. She had lost the inner battle almost before it had begun.

She lifted her hips slightly as he tenderly pulled her slacks down and tossed them into a corner. Gently, gently, he tugged at her lacy panties until they too joined the heap. She lay there for a moment, watching Gus's face as he took her in, looked at her with unmistakable desire. Still, she held back—she simply wasn't ready to give in, not yet, not this easily.

He stood up to remove his slacks, his fingers fumbling in anticipation for a moment at the belt buckle. Then they too joined the tumble of clothes in the corner, and soon his shorts followed suit. He stood there for a moment, letting Madeline look at him, and suddenly she realized that he was giving her time to think, time to stop. But she knew she couldn't. There was something about Gus standing there, waiting for her, that made her reach out a hand to pull him down beside her. She would ask questions later. Right now she seemed to have only answers.

Gus tumbled gracefully down beside her, his body stretched out next to hers on the huge bed. One hand gracefully snaked out and stroked her entire length. Madeline turned on one side, resting on one elbow, watching him watch her. It was an easy, tentative touch, and she knew that he was still giving her a chance. But suddenly it all seemed clear to her—she and Gus had been moving toward this moment the entire time. She smiled at him, her lips parted provocatively, letting him know that there would be no turning back. Then she reached for his mouth with her lips, as if making the first move would banish the chance to resist.

As though he sensed what she was thinking, Gus reached out an arm and pulled her close in a fierce embrace, crushing her lips to his. There would be no turning back now, she could see that. She could feel it in the urgency of his embrace. His mouth descended once again to her breasts, while his hands teased her tender flesh, tracing a line along her waist, finally reaching lower and lower, yet so slowly that Madeline thought she'd never experienced such exquisite torment. Gus knew what would please her, and when his mouth grazed the tender flesh of her lower stomach, she could only urge him onward, holding on to his dark hair, twisting, writhing under his firm exploratory kisses.

Finally, the kisses were no longer exploratory. Gus had found what he was looking for and his lips sought her hungrily. Madeline twisted and turned against the tortuous rhythms of his tongue and finally she couldn't stand it anymore. "I want you," she told him. "I want you so badly."

Gus towered over her for an instant, then gently, ever so gently joined with her, as if he wanted to prolong that first moment of union forever. Inch by inch, Madeline could feel herself giving in, reaching for him, and becoming his. She reveled in the sensation of his rough chest against the smooth skin of her breasts and she was surprised to find that her response to Gus was quick and immediate. Nothing like this had ever happened before.

Gus, for his part, continued to love her, to stroke her fiercely once again toward the crest. He seemd tireless in his efforts to arouse her further, and he showed incredible self-control, as if he wanted her to know how much he wanted to please her. Finally, she could feel her passion rising to an uncontrollable level and Madeline spurred him onward, her nails grazing his back, urging him to go on, letting him know how much she wanted him.

The final movement was as fierce and fiery as the beginning had been sweet and tender. Locked together, they arched toward each other simultaneously in a moment of dizzying sensation. Madeline cried out his name, and he responded by pulling her close, holding her against him as if he would never let her go. When it was all over, he lay beside her, stroking her face with his finger, gently tracing the outline of each feature.

"Didn't I tell you we belong together?" he asked, wrapping her up in his strong arms.

"Yes, you did," Madeline said, snuggling up beside him. She was already slipping close to the edge of sleep. "And I should have known you'd be the kind of person who'd say 'I told you so.'"

"That's right," Gus said with a sleepy smile. "I told you so."

5

Without moving, Madeline opened her eyes slow-ly, then closed them again against the cruel light of day. She turned over, wide awake this time, her gray eyes surveying the strange room. For a mo-ment, she didn't know where she was. Everything looked different in broad daylight. Then the sleep-ing form beside her moved, snuggling up close, and it all came back—the drive-in movie, the grand piano, *Forbidden Stars* and the man who wrote the music. She had surrendered completely to the moment, to the music and the man. She groaned softly to herself, her good sense taking charge once again. How could she have been so reckless?

She glanced at her wristwatch on the nightstand. It was six o'clock. At least she hadn't overslept. Thank goodness for small favors, she thought to herself sardonically, slipping out of bed. Too bad other disciplines weren't so automatic. She turned to look at Gus still sleeping, his breath slow and even. His arms were tucked around a pillow and his handsome, rugged features were somehow boyish, while his enormous energies lay dormant. Madeline knew she couldn't waste time, knew she had to tear herself away. It was too late for circumspection, too late to undo what had happened the night before.

Picking her rumpled white smock up off the floor, she was furious with herself. Now that the night had passed, she was able to see what she had been blind to only a few hours before—the twenty-twenty vision of hindsight, she thought glumly, slipping her arms through the long full sleeves of the blouse, then reaching for her slacks. She padded softly on bare feet to the bathroom. And it would be today of all days! A photographer from *Houston Homes* was coming over to photograph her apartment for the magazine, something Madeline had tried to get out of. But Mamie had insisted she do it, because the photographer was a friend of hers. Madeline wasn't worried about the apartment, of course, but she was beginning to understand what it meant to live in a glass house. She wasn't used to being so much in the public eye.

Bending over the sink, she threw some cold water on her face and throat. It didn't help. The profound remorse she felt this morning wouldn't be so easily washed away. She looked at her face in the mirror, her gray eyes still sleepy, her cheeks flushed, her long black hair cascading around her shoulders. She looked like a woman who had just been made love to, and very thoroughly at that.

How could she have been so irresponsible? She

had a professional relationship with this man as well as an obligation to the symphony. Under these circumstances, she felt that her judgment about his music could certainly be called into question. How much of her love for the music was the powerful physical attraction she felt for the man? She had traveled this road before, she thought bitterly, remembering Martin Singer and the love affair that had left her heart broken for longer than she cared to admit. She had been as much in love with his music as she had been with the man himself, and she had let herself be swept away by both. Everything she'd valued, everything she'd spent a lifetime working for, was pushed aside, and she'd lost her own identity, all sense of herself. She'd vowed then never to let her work get tangled up with the affairs of the heart. So what happened last night? What on earth could she have been thinking of?

As much as she hated to admit it, she knew that there was a very good reason for her surrender. She'd been alone so long, so dedicated to her new responsibilities, that she'd starved herself emotionally. She'd been hungry for someone like Gus, hungry for a shared personal moment. The fact that he was handsome and fun and talented only made him harder to resist. She tiptoed back to the bedroom door, unable to resist another look. She longed to crawl back into bed with him, pull him close, wake him with a kiss. You can't have it all, Madeline, she reminded herself firmly. Forget it.

She hastily gathered up her belongings, which were scattered everywhere, moving quietly so as not to disturb him. As she passed through the living room, she stopped for a moment at the piano, trailing her fingers soundlessly along the ivory keys, her eyes resting on the scattered pages of the score. The music was good, she reminded herself, better than good, and she would do whatever she could to make it work. That's what mattered. She stooped automatically to retrieve a stray piece of paper, placing it carefully on the coffee table. Impulsively, she carried the two wineglasses to the kitchen. What are you trying to do, Markey, she chided herself—remove the evidence? Pretend it didn't happen? Or stay a little longer?

She was quietly unlatching the chain lock on the door when the phone rang in the living room. She froze, not sure what to do. If she let it ring, Gus would wake up and find out she was leaving. If she answered it, she'd have to take a message. She hesitated a brief second, then hurried to the phone. "Hello," she said softly.

"I'm sorry, I must have the wrong number. I'm trying to reach Gus Noble." Madeline felt her heart sink when she realized it was Mamie's voice. She didn't know what to do. "Hello?" Mamie said, questioningly.

"Just a moment, I'll put him on." Madeline started to put the phone down, but Mamie called her name.

"Madeline, is that you?" The question was a little uncertain, and Mamie sounded puzzled.

"Yes," she admitted. She could have kicked herself, especially when she saw Gus standing in the doorway stretching, his eyes sleepy and inquisitive. "I'll see you later this morning, Mamie," she said, and held out the phone to him.

He took it, but gave her a brief hard kiss before

speaking into the receiver. "Good morning Mamie," he said. "You're calling awfully early. I thought we were having lunch tomorrow." Madeline retreated toward the kitchen, not wanting to eavesdrop. She shouldn't have answered the phone. Mamie could think only one thing, reaching her in Gus's hotel room this early in the morning. And she'd be right. Madeline's face flushed crimson as she realized she would have to face the board member in only a few hours. What would she say?

Filled with nervous energy, she looked around for something to do. She had just turned on the hot water to wash the wineglasses when she heard Gus come into the small room. Not sure she could face him, she played with the faucets, pretending to be looking for the soap. He came up behind her, turned off the faucet, then put his arms around her, his lips lightly brushing the back of her neck in a feather kiss.

"Good morning," he said softly, his lips trailing across her shoulder.

She felt a fleeting impulse to give in, to lean back and be swallowed up by the rush of physical pleasure she was feeling, but she knew that she couldn't. She'd already made one big mistake, and she'd be damned if she'd do it again. She turned to face him, the smile on her face artificial and strained. "Good morning," she said brightly. "I'm sorry the phone woke you."

"I see it didn't wake you," Gus pointed out, noticing that she was fully dressed. Madeline was sure that he'd seen her purse on the table as well. "Going somewhere?"

"I didn't want to disturb you," she explained a

bit lamely, then hurried on. "A photographer from *Houston Homes* is coming over with Mamie to take pictures of my apartment this morning and I thought I'd better get over there. And you were still sleeping and it's still early. . . ." Her voice trailed off uncertainly.

"That would be a cute trick," Gus said, and his voice was a little harsh. "You need a ride, remember? And it would also be a way to go home without facing me, is that it? I don't suppose you were going to leave a note?" He searched her face for the answer. "Come on in and talk to me while I get dressed. Then I'll drive you home."

Madeline followed him into the bedroom, not wanting to push, but desperately wondering what he'd told Mamie. She watched with embarrassment while Gus matter-of-factly pulled on his clothes, as if dressing in front of her was something he did every day. She couldn't help but admire his powerful physique, remembering what it was like to be held in his arms, to feel his body close to hers. For a moment, she forgot to worry about future repercussions. She only wanted to stay here with him.

"I'm sorry about Mamie," Gus began, but Madeline interrupted him.

"Don't be," she said firmly. "I had no business answering your phone. I'm sorry it put you in an awkward position."

"Me?" he said in amazement. "I'm sorry you were put on the spot." He buttoned up his shirt, then went on. "I told her we'd been working."

Madeline laughed at the man's sheer nerve. Well, it was partly true.

"What's so funny?" he demanded. "Musicians

are notorious for their strange hours, aren't they?" She had to hand it to him, he seemed cool as could be.

"And what did she say?" Madeline asked curiously, feeling a little less tense. "Did she believe you?"

"I don't know," Gus replied, his voice muffled as he leaned over to tie his shoes. "She said she was glad we were getting along so well, whatever that means." He sat up and looked her straight in the eye. "Does it matter that much to you?"

She sat back in the chair, her spine stiff and straight. "Yes, it does. I'm still new in Houston, remember, and Mamie played an important part in bringing me here. I don't want to let her down."

Gus stood up and walked over to her, taking her hands and pulling her to her feet, his arms going around her to hold her close. "The only way you could let her down, Markey, is to be not as talented as you are. What you do on your own time is your own business. You're a conductor, not an indentured servant, for God's sake." He held her by the shoulders, standing back a bit, looking into her eyes. "And last night was between us. What happened is our business."

Madeline saw that he was going to kiss her, but she stepped aside adroitly, not wanting her body to betray her. She didn't have much time. "Business," she said firmly. "That's what we should have been doing. Not falling into bed together."

"We didn't exactly fall into bed," Gus pointed out. "We walked there—each of us on our own two feet and with our eyes wide open. I don't understand why you're acting this way." He seemed on the edge of anger, and Markey could easily understand why, but she just couldn't let herself go. That had been her mistake in the first place.

"I'm sorry, Gus," she said finally. "I have to go home. I'm going to be cutting it close as it is. Last night was really special, I agree, and I'm sorry this morning got started this way. I really am." But she knew in her heart that it was just as well that she had to face the consequences of her actions. Better to come to terms with them now than later.

Gus seemed to sense her determination, for he appeared ready to drop the subject temporarily. "I'll run you home," he said, brushing her cheek in a kiss. "Let's get going. I didn't mean to pin you down. We have all the time in the world for talking."

He reached for his car keys and she followed him out the door, carrying a copy of his score that he'd given her. Once they reached the outside she took in a deep breath; the clear, cool air was refreshing. It was a new day, she reminded herself. Every day could be a new start. She stole a sidelong glance at Gus. He certainly seemed to be happy. They drove the few short blocks to her apartment, talking easily about the weather and the city, ignoring the loaded issue of their night together. When they pulled up to the door of 1400 Hermann, Markey was surprised when Gus parked the car and got out.

She stepped out of the car, then looked up at him. "Aren't you leaving?" Then, realizing how the words must sound, she hurried to add, "Or would you like to come up for a cup of coffee?"

"Coffee would be great," Gus said firmly, following her into the building for the short elevator ride to her apartment. "No wonder I'm moving so slowly this morning. Haven't had a drop yet."

Madeline opened the door to her apartment and hurried to the kitchen, quickly plugging in the automatic coffee maker. She hoped he'd leave soon, not that she wanted to rush him out, but surely he would understand that he couldn't stay. "Do you mind if I take a shower?" she asked, as the coffee began to drip.

"No, go ahead," Gus called again from the living room, where he was examining her collection of musical instruments. "I'll make myself at home." At Markey's slightly alarmed look, he added. "Don't worry. I won't break anything."

This is silly, she said to herself as she headed for the bathroom. The cold shower was wonderfully refreshing and afterward she felt like a new person. The troubles of the morning seemed more manageable now. It wasn't like her to run away from her problems, but she still felt that it was going to be hard to deal with Gus. The man was special; what they'd shared had been wonderful; but it couldn't continue. It had been an impulsive moment, romantic to be sure, but romance was going to have to take a back seat in the future.

She dried herself quickly and slipped on a long, white Mexican wedding dress richly embroidered and detailed in heavy white lace. She tied back her hair with a wide pink ribbon, letting the long black curls fall to her shoulders. Now she was beginning to think a little more clearly. The vague regret that had slapped her in the face earlier was beginning to take the shape of a number of practical considerations. She was new in Houston, with an important position that kept her in the public eye, and she wanted to stay here, wanted to take advantage of this opportunity. Gus was only here to make a movie, to see his music produced, then he'd be going back to Hollywood, half a continent away. There was no future in this relationship—and a wonderful present wasn't worth sacrificing the dream of a lifetime. Those were the simple facts of the matter.

The smell of fresh coffee permeated the air and Madeline made her way back to the kitchen, following the enticing aroma. Coffee was what she needed. She poured herself a cup and went off to find Gus, who was on the balcony overlooking Hermann Park's Rose Garden, and beyond that, Miller Theater.

"This is a nice place you have here," he said appreciatively. "I love your collection." He gestured toward the musical instruments. "How did you ever find them all?"

"My father is a diplomat, and we've lived all over the world. Most of them are souvenirs." She looked over at him, noticing that his face was thoughtful. Only half an hour before Mamie came. Certainly he wasn't planning to stay. "Well," she suggested, "you've had your coffee."

"What?" he asked. "Don't you want me to stay and say hello to Mamie? Tell her about how hard we worked?" His voice was teasing, but Madeline was afraid he might be serious.

"I think that might be awkward," she began cautiously. "After all, she's coming with a photographer who's a friend of hers to take pictures of the apartment."

Gus stood up and walked over to the railing of the balcony. "What's the matter, Markey? Afraid to be seen with someone in your ivory tower here? Aren't you supposed to have friends, let alone lovers?" He turned back to her, his face set. "And I don't want us just to have been lovers once. You know that there was more to what happened last night than just physical attraction. A lot more. Why are you running away from it?"

"I'm not running away from it," she insisted. "I just don't see the need to broadcast it, that's all. I'm worried enough about this morning—and I would be even if we hadn't been together last night. It's hard to have your home on display for the public. That's enough to put me on edge. And to make matters worse, you practically want to shout the news from the rooftops that we spent last night together!" The minutes were ticking by and she was beginning to feel more and more trapped.

"All right," Gus said, slamming his coffee cup down on the small glass tabletop. "I *would* like to shout it from the rooftops." He groaned when he saw the coffee slosh onto her dress. "God, I'm sorry. I'm really making a mess of this. I'll go—but first let me help you clean this up."

Madeline had already gotten up and was about to head for the kitchen. "Don't worry, I'll get it. Just go, all right?" Only fifteen minutes.

Gus took a dish towel and soaked it in cold water, then began dabbing at her dress. "It's coming out, see?"

"I'll have to change," she said frantically. "Look —would you do me a favor and clean off the table. Then leave? Please!"

"All right," Gus said. "I can see I'm only making this harder." He grabbed the towel and headed for the balcony while Madeline went to the bedroom to change. When she came back, he was in the kitchen, which was now neat as a pin, coffee cups washed and put away. "I'm sorry," he said. "We'll talk later. Maybe tonight. How about dinner?"

"Call me," Madeline said firmly, tucking her pink silk shirt into her tailored gray slacks and leading him to the door. "Just call me."

"I will," Gus promised, leaning forward to claim her mouth in a hard, fast kiss. "Count on it." He opened the door and went out.

Madeline leaned against the closed door with a sigh of relief. She felt like an actress in a situation comedy who'd just had a narrow escape. Taking a deep breath, she hurried through the apartment for a final once-over, arranging irises in a tall crystal vase on the glass coffee table, adjusting the arrangement of her collection of musical instruments, fluffing the lavender pillows on the white sofa. When the next knock came, she was ready.

"Good morning, Markey," Mamie said, ushering in a tall woman who was burdened with camera equipment. "I'd like you to meet my friend Sally Jennings, from *Houston Homes.*" She turned to the tall redhead who'd stacked her things in the middle of the room. "Sally, this is Madeline Mark, our new conductor."

"What a place!" Sally said admiringly, looking around the room. "This is going to be fun." She paused, as if remembering her manners. "Pleased to meet you, Ms. Mark. Call me Sally."

Madeline shook hands graciously. "Call me

Markey. And make yourself at home. Coffee?" She looked at the two women.

Mamie nodded, but Sally was already starting to set up her equipment. "Maybe later."

Madeline went into the kitchen and poured Mamie a cup of coffee, glad that Sally was there as a buffer. The photographer was so enthusiastic that she thought she might almost enjoy this. But Mamie seemed a little ill at ease, and Madeline wanted to say something to her to clear the air.

She walked back into the living room where Sally was already snapping away, taking pictures of the room from every conceivable angle. Mamie was watching her, making a comment now and then, and she smiled her thanks as she accepted the steaming cup.

"Sally, can I do anything to help?" Madeline offered, though it looked like she'd only be in the way.

"Oh, I'll have a few questions for you later, and then I'll want a few pictures of you—maybe at the piano, but for now you can relax. Why don't you and Mamie go out on the balcony and enjoy your coffee? I'll call you when I'm ready for you." Sally turned back to her work.

"Shall we?" With some dread, Madeline led the way out to the balcony, gesturing Mamie to take a seat at the small table. It seemed that the moment was upon them. "Isn't it lovely out here?"

"I'm glad you like it," Mamie said pleasantly. "I've always thought this was a lovely building. And it's perfect for you when we do concerts in the park." She sipped her coffee.

Madeline suddenly knew that she had to say

something, anything to break the artificial atmosphere of this conversation. Mamie was too shrewd and Madeline owed her too much. "Mamie, about this morning—"

Mamie put her cup down and leaned forward, folding her hands together and resting them on the edge of the table. "Not to worry, Markey," she said firmly. "If you were working, you were working, I can understand that. But I would like to point out something."

While Madeline wasn't quite sure she could relax, she was glad Mamie was being so direct. "What's that?" she asked politely.

"I worked very hard to convince the board that you were the right person for this position. You are very talented, but you are still very young, and of course, there was a lot of resistance to the idea of a woman conductor. You're doing a good job. But never forget that you are constantly in the public eye, and that your job carries with it an important social responsibility. What you do on your own time is your business, of course. I would only suggest that you be discreet." Mamie sat back in her wrought-iron chair and reached for her coffee.

"I will," Madeline said evenly. "Thank you." Part of her knew that Mamie was giving good advice, and doing it gracefully, but part of her resented being in such a situation at all. She had to give Mamie her due—answering the phone in a man's hotel room early in the morning was hardly discreet—even if they had only been working. Appearances were important, a lesson she'd learned long ago as a member of a diplomatic family. She'd just have to remember it.

"Hold it right there!" Sally called from the open doorway. "I'll take this one for you. You look so nice out there, two friends chatting over their morning coffee."

Madeline smiled automatically over at Mamie, and both women looked toward the camera. She knew that she was going to have to make some changes. She was going to have to remind herself every day that she and Gus had no future, no relationship beyond a professional one. One way to keep from making mistakes was not to repeat them.

The rest of the photography session was easy and pleasant, and Madeline enjoyed giving the two other women the history of her collection. Seeing her new apartment through Sally's eyes made her appreciate it even more, made her realize that she was really beginning to regard Houston as her home. When the two women left, she was actually sorry, for the morning had flown by.

She was just getting ready to leave for the office downtown when the phone rang. "All clear?" Gus laughed. "I called about dinner, but I can always call back later. How did things go?"

"Very well, thank you," Madeline said a bit stiffly. "And yes, they've gone. Everything was fine."

"Great!" Gus seemed to hesitate for a second. "Well, what about tonight?"

Madeline absently zipped and unzipped her purse as she thought of the best way to say the difficult words. "Look, Gus," she finally explained, "this can't work. You and I have a professional relationship and that's all it can ever be. Last night was an impulsive mistake and while I honestly can't say I'm sorry it happened, I have to make sure that it doesn't happen again. That's just the way it has to be."

There was a long silence. "What did Mamie say?" Gus demanded. "Is that it? I'm having lunch with her tomorrow, you know, and I'm perfectly willing to tell her to mind her own business."

She knew he was capable of doing just that and it was the last thing she wanted. "It wasn't Mamie," she insisted. "It's me. I can't handle this right now. I have enough adjustments to make without adding a new relationship. Don't you see that all you can do for me is complicate my life?"

"And you like it simple," Gus said sarcastically. "Neat and simple. Scared little thing, aren't you?"

Now she felt angry. "Not scared, Gus. Just determined. I'll work with you and I'll enjoy that," she promised. "But nothing more. Don't even ask."

"I'd never ask for something you weren't ready to give, Markey," he returned quietly, the anger gone from his voice, replaced by resignation. "All right. Have it your way. For now." He hung up the phone.

Madeline replaced the receiver and stared at it for a long silent moment. It had been so hard to tell him that, when what she really wanted to say was yes, let's have dinner, yes, I want to see you. She knew that she had to be careful, but her heart ached at the cost; she realized for the first time how lonely she was. What she had shared with Gus had only been a temporary island of closeness and companionship. But they couldn't be lovers, she reminded herself firmly. They'd have to be friends if that was possible. Still, she couldn't help thinking about the memory of his touch, his kiss.

You shouldn't want what you can't have, she told herself firmly, heading for the door. And what you have right now is a job to do. Never forget that. She had her hand on the knob when she realized that she didn't even have a way to get to the office. Her car was still in its parking space back at Jones Hall.

"Damn!" she swore softly, heading back toward the phone to call a taxi. She was angry with herself for being caught in this position. Just remember this later, she told herself sadly. Never let this happen again.

Despite her resolution, she could feel tears coming to her eyes. Why did everything have to be so hard? Why couldn't she have Gus and the job she loved too? The little bit of love had made her hungry for more, and she wondered for the first time if she was really satisfied. Now that she'd gotten her dream, she hoped it would be enough. But what about Gus? Had she gotten one dream only to run away from another?

6

Madeline slowly let her arms drop to her sides after the orchestra had finished the final measure of Beethoven's Third Symphony. She was tired. The rehearsal that morning had been good but long. There was still the afternoon to get through and she felt stretched to her limit. She gestured for everyone's attention. "All right, let's take a lunch break," she called out. "You did well this morning. Let's see how you do this afternoon. Meet back here in an hour, ready to work on *Forbidden Stars.*"

Madeline walked down the side steps of the stage and gratefully sank into a front-row seat. Up on stage, the orchestra was getting ready to depart for lunch. "Markey, do you want to come to the Mexicatessen with us?" Figaro asked. "You look like you could use a few hot peppers to spice you up."

"Yes, come with us," Angel added.

"No thanks, I brought a sandwich." Madeline wanted to go with them, but she knew she had to save her energy for the rehearsal that afternoon. She always worked on a delicate balance of tension and calm, and she knew that to relax right now might mean she wouldn't be able to pull herself together again.

Figaro and Angel went off with the others, leaving Madeline alone in the auditorium. She went up to the symphony offices to get a soft drink out of the refrigerator, then came back down to look over the pages of the score for that afternoon. She was lost in thought, munching a turkey-and-avocado sandwich, when she felt a warm breath on her shoulder.

"You're working too hard," Gus said in a reproachful voice. "You didn't even hear me come in."

Madeline turned to look at him, her pleasure mixed with momentary dismay. Ever since that night she and Gus had been lovers, she had always felt awkward about seeing him. He had respected her wish, though not without some displeasure, that their relationship remain a professional one. That was not the problem. The problem was that she could scarcely think about anything else. She dreamed about Gus. He was her first waking thought in the morning, the last at night. She told herself this was only a reflection of the loneliness of her position, that it had nothing to do with Gus, not really. But she didn't often fool herself, not for long. Now she saw his dark curly hair and wanted to reach out and run her fingers through it. She looked into his dark eyes and wanted to smile into them. And when she thought of his mouth, she . .

With an effort of will, she snapped back to attention. "I would have heard you come in," she said, "if you hadn't been sneaking around." He was dressed as he usually was for rehearsals, in jeans, a casual shirt and sports coat, a pair of white running shoes.

"I'm not sneaking around," Gus answered with a touch of mock indignation. He looked down at his feet. "It's my running shoes. People never hear me coming and suddenly I'm there. Always an entrance."

That was certainly true for the way Gus had come into her life, Madeline thought. All of a sudden, one day he was there, with no warning, an important part of her world. They had seen each other only professionally during the recent days of his stay in Houston, and she had been relieved that he was so busy with the other things. It had given them both a cooling-off period, and for that Madeline had been grateful. At first, Gus's business in Houston had not involved her much. Brew had handled the business end of the deal, which had required some patient negotiations with the movie company. Then, while the movie itself was being finished, Gus had been busy with that. But, when the orchestra started rehearsals the last week of September, Gus had been around almost constantly. Madeline had found it increasingly difficult to maintain a professional attitude about him. Even when he had been busy with other things, Gus had dropped by or called her at least once a week, and she had soon realized that she was looking forward to these short visits. Now that he had to be at Jones Hall every day, the tension between them had mounted; it took all of her professional acumen to keep her distance. And she didn't know how long she could keep this up.

"Well, since you're here," she allowed with a forced smile, "what can I do for you?"

"Two things," Gus announced with gusto. "You can let me watch the rehearsal this afternoon, and you can have dinner with me tonight."

Madeline finished up her sandwich and dusted whole wheat crumbs from her fingertips. "You can certainly watch the rehearsals today, like you always do," she said, "but I've got too much work to do tonight. I can't go out."

"Can't or won't?" His voice was suddenly harsh.

"It doesn't matter," Madeline said, without meeting his eyes directly. "In either case, the answer is no."

Gus lowered his voice as he continued the argument. "You can't keep on playing this cat-and-mouse game with me, Markey. I don't like it. I know it's not good for me, and it can't be good for you either."

"I'll be the judge of what's good for me, if you don't mind," Madeline returned a bit stiffly. She knew what he was saying was perfectly true. The situation wasn't fair to either of them, but she simply felt that she could do it no other way. "I'm doing my best to do justice to your work, Gus. Don't pretend you're a pampered artist who needs to be coddled. The work is the most important thing right now." She sighed. "We've been through this before."

Gus shoved his hands in his pockets and considered her thoughtfully for a few seconds. "All right, Markey, work it is. I promised you that and I'll keep my word. How about calling it a working dinner? After all, we have a lot to go over before the recording session. There are a thousand things I need to explain to you."

Madeline knew there was some truth to that. And she also knew she would have to meet with him at night for this sort of detail. Her days were simply too full. "A working dinner?" She looked up at him skeptically, knowing she was going to say yes.

"Scout's honor," Gus assured her, holding up two fingers as a pledge.

"I don't believe for a minute that you were ever a Boy Scout, Gus Noble!" Madeline fired back with a trace of her usual good humor. "But I'm not sure I have much of a choice," she added shortly. "Make it late. I really do have a lot of work to do tonight, and after this rehearsal, I have a meeting with Brew to work on the schedule for the tour. How about eight-thirty? You can pick me up at my place."

"It's a date," Gus said eagerly. "I won't bother you after rehearsal, either. We'll just talk tonight."

"Deal," Madeline said firmly, pleased in spite of herself at the prospect of seeing him. She stood up, stuffing her lunch wrapping into a paper bag. "Now, if you'll excuse me."

"See you later." Gus started to walk away. "I think I'll take a seat in one of the balconies. I like hearing what the acoustics are like up there."

"You do that," Madeline said absently. Her attention was already returning to the work ahead of her. She didn't want to think too much about

Gus being there, watching. It would throw off her concentration. He had that effect on her most of the time, she thought ruefully, and she certainly didn't want to feel that way during rehearsal.

She turned the pages of the score once again, thinking ahead to the work for the afternoon. Everything was shaping up fairly well. The orchestra had given no real objection to the increased work load. No, the score for *Forbidden Stars* was no problem. Madeline's only real problem at the moment was Maurice. He hadn't been to rehearsal for the past three days. He hadn't even called in to say he was sick, and no one knew where he was. Figaro and Angel were also worried, and had said so quite frankly a couple of nights ago when the three of them went out for a drink with Brew after a performance.

"It's his parents," Figaro had explained, shaking his head doubtfully. "They don't approve of his dating a Vietnamese. They're making life pretty unpleasant for him, I think, even threatening to cut off his inheritance if he continues to see her."

"Can you imagine such prejudice?" Angel had said sympathetically. "Thui's an absolutely beautiful woman. I met her one night last summer when Maurice took me over to Mai Que, the Vietnamese restaurant where she works. I like her a lot, and Maurice is head over heels in love with her. I just don't know what he's going to do."

"Well, that explains a lot," Madeline had murmured, as much to herself as to the others. She had known that Maurice came from a wealthy family, an only child in fact, and her heart went out to him.

An unhappy love affair, as she well knew, could be crippling, all consuming. Somehow she had to help him. If only he would talk to her about it, if only he would trust her enough to explain his unhappiness . . . somehow she had to reach him. He couldn't keep on like this, whatever the reason, and sooner or later she would have to give him an official reprimand. But he was a fine musician. She didn't want to lose him. It wasn't an easy problem.

Brew had let out a cloud of smoke, and looked around thoughtfully. "Maurice is young. He'll come out of it, I'm sure. I just hope he doesn't give up everything else that's important to him. Romance isn't everything, you know."

"I know," Madeline had concurred, glad to hear the concern in his voice, "but I think we'd have a hard time convincing Maurice of that right now. Love may not be everything but it sure has a way of taking over."

"Something tells me you're going to be a big help to Maurice," Brew had said fondly, adjusting his bow tie. "You're smart—about music and about people."

"I wish that were always the case," Madeline had said wistfully. She'd been thinking about Gus, knowing that she wasn't handling the situation with him as well as she'd like to be. She was afraid of falling in love with him, and that's exactly what she couldn't let happen. Someday, *Forbidden Stars* would be over, and he would leave. And soon, maybe even before that, she would be leaving for Europe with the orchestra. No sense giving your heart when you know you're going to get it back eventually, she'd reminded herself firmly. Be careful.

"Ms. Mark?" Angel's voice brought her back to the present. "Did you eat lunch?"

"Yes, I did," Madeline answered, holding up the brown paper sack. "This is all that remains of a wonderful sandwich."

"Good." The girl smiled. "We missed you. I can't tell you how much we're all looking forward to doing the piece again this afternoon. This soundtrack is really exciting."

"It is wonderful music, isn't it?" Madeline was glad that the orchestra seemed to think as much of Gus's work as she did. It only validated her choice. And most of them were equally excited about the extra money. Not only were they making enough money for the European tour, but all of the musicians were taking home a sizable chunk as well. Financially, it was a good arrangement all around.

Madeline gave Angel a wink and went over to the podium. "Now, let's give some time to the symphony for *Forbidden Stars,*" she announced. "We've only got another month for this one, and I want to be sure we're ready."

The orchestra had been working on the piece for a few weeks now, and Madeline was pleased with the progress they were making. Though she suspected that all of them had had initial doubts about it, now they all seemed to accept it as a challenge. First and foremost, the music swept them away. If it hadn't, no amount of money could have coaxed a good performance out of them. She also knew that her own enthusiasm for the work made a lot of difference. When she had told Brewster of her decision that crazy morning in July, he had been pleased and surprised by her sudden change of heart.

"You're sure I'm not pushing you into anything?" he had asked. "Mamie Spencer has some wonderful ideas, but if you really don't want to do this, I can put a stop to it."

"Oh, no, Brew," she'd assured him. "Gus's music is intelligent, sensitive, often brilliant. I feel sure the orchestra will like it as much as I do."

And they had. Once the contracts had been signed, she'd given Gus a couple of hours with the orchestra to explain the plot of the movie and what he meant for the music to do, and she had known then that it would be all right. The musicians had all been captivated, and they had set to work eagerly. She was only sorry that they had to concentrate on other things as well. So many things had to be done at the same time: rehearsals for the regular season and for the tour, auditions and performances. In spite of the increased workload however, it was all coming together.

Today was no exception. Even the more modern parts of the work, which had originally given the orchestra the most trouble, were starting to sound as they were meant to. The star theme—ah, that was another matter—had been almost perfect from the beginning. And, though it was not easy for her, Madeline also suspected that Gus's presence at rehearsals made all the difference. The women, in particular, were charmed by him. Madeline had rarely seen a composer so well accepted by the orchestra. It was a challenge for the musicians to play Gus's own work to his satisfaction, a challenge they met with courage and excitement.

As they finished playing the piece for the second time, Madeline felt encouraged. Another month or so and she would be satisfied. A date still hadn't been set for the actual recording, but Gus had told her to be ready by the end of November. That didn't seem unrealistic, though the production of this soundtrack had been added to an already busy schedule.

As she dismissed the orchestra with a few final notes to individuals, she turned around, half-expecting to see Gus coming down the aisle. But to her surprise, he seemed to have disappeared. Instead, Brew Baker was rapidly approaching with a concerned look on his face.

"Can I see you for a few moments, Markey?" he asked.

"Sure," she said easily. "I'll be right up. A problem?"

"I hope not," Brew said tersely. "I'll wait for you in my office."

Madeline frowned. It wasn't like Brew to be so short with her. She hoped it wasn't anything personal. She got her things together and went up to the manager's office as soon as she could.

"What's going on?" she demanded as soon as she entered the room. She relaxed a bit when she saw that Brew was in the office chair behind the desk, his feet propped up on the desk top. It couldn't be too serious. "Is it something about the tour?"

"No, no, Markey, not the tour. That's all set. All

we have to do is finish out the fall season, then you'll be off to Athens, the first stop. No, that's not the problem." He paused and looked at her speculatively. "It's the recording for *Forbidden Stars.*"

"What about it?" Markey had the feeling that she was about to get her deadline.

"It's been pushed up to the second week in November." Brew's expression was for the most part noncommittal, though she could detect the question in his mind. Could they be ready?

"I thought we'd have at least another month!" It wasn't impossible, Madeline knew, but she was under enough pressure already. And so were the musicians!

"I know. Can we be ready?"

Madeline knew Brew would respect her answer. She thought for a moment, trying to weigh the different alternatives, but there didn't seem to be any. "We'll have to be," she said crisply. "I would have appreciated a little more time, but I feel sure we can pull it together. We're pretty close as it is. Besides," she added resolutely, "the sooner we get this over with, the better."

"That's the spirit!" Brew smiled, as if he had known she would react that way.

"All right." Madeline was thinking fast. "Please type up notices of the location and the times for recording—whatever the musicians need. If you could have them ready by next week, that would be great."

The next hour passed quickly as she and Brew discussed the problems of the logistics involved. The sound stage was in a rather remote part of Houston, and though she had been there twice with Gus while the movie was actually being shot and edited, she knew that it would take an extra effort for the members of the orchestra to get there. Once there, they'd all have to have special passes to be allowed into the complex. Then they faced the difficult part—the recording itself. Madeline was just familiar enough with the process to be nervous about it. It was one thing to make music for a regularly scheduled live performance, another to record music, and still more complicated to try to match up the process with the film itself. Gus would go over it all with her, of course. When the time came, he'd be there to guide her through it.

"Gus!" Madeline thought suddenly. "Did he know about this?" She knew she'd been short with him at rehearsal. Maybe he'd been trying to tell her about it when she'd cut him off. Maybe he was planning to tell her about it at dinner. If not, he'd be even more surprised than she was.

"Well, he didn't know about it until I told him," Brew admitted. "The studio called my office looking for him and I sent the secretary downstairs to get him. He took the call in my office."

"Did he seem worried?" Madeline was genuinely curious. She wondered how much of the rehearsal he'd been able to hear.

"Not a bit." Brew smiled a self-satisfied smile. "In that respect, you two are a lot alike. He's just as anxious to get his music scored for the film as you are to get the whole thing over with before the tour. He didn't seem at all concerned."

"Good." Madeline was relieved. Getting ready to leave, she said, "Thanks, Brew. I'll tell the orchestra about it this afternoon if you'll get all the details in writing for them." By the time she left the office, she was feeling pretty optimistic. They were cutting it a little too close for her tastes, but she knew she could always call a few extra rehearsals—the studio would pay for it. But she didn't want to overwork the orchestra. They had the regularly scheduled performances in addition to rehearsing for the European tour. Well, they could do it. They were good musicians, all of them. The best. She was proud of her orchestra and she knew they would do well—even under circumstances which were not ideal.

By the time she got home, she was feeling even more relaxed. There was, after all, nothing she could really do about it. And she knew that the music was coming along as well as could be expected by this point.

She poured herself a tall drink of mineral water and lime and walked out onto the balcony overlooking the park. Houston was still hot—even in October—and she couldn't help remembering that Fourth of July concert and the night she'd first met Gus. It seemed so long ago, in some respects, but on the other hand, so much had happened so quickly. Already she was dealing with the crushing realization that it would be over soon. Once the soundtrack was finished, there would be nothing to keep Gus in Houston. He would go back to his house in Malibu and write more songs, and wait for the next call from a movie studio. He would be out of her life forever.

Madeline took a long, slow drink of the bubbling water and went back into the cool living room with its elegant white furniture and touches of lavender and gray. This was her room, she reflected, this was the room where her real life was. Her ivory tower, Gus had called it. She looked around at her collection of antique musical instruments, remembering Gus's lively curiosity in each and every one of them. Still, her real life would go on here long after he had gone back to his. She'd just have to be careful. Thank goodness she had had the good sense not to have more than a professional relationship with Gus. At least she had protected herself a bit.

The doorbell rang promptly at eight-thirty. By then she had showered and changed into a cool, flowing, gray and white geometric print dress. She had piled her hair loosely on top of her head, allowing a few tendrils to curl loosely around her face. That had been one of the few benefits of Houston's oppressive humidity, she thought. Even her normally straight hair would sometimes spring to life.

"Hi!" she said breezily, opening the door to Gus. She didn't want him to know that she was at all concerned about the rushed recording date.

"You look great," he said, his bold eyes drinking her in. "I'm not sure I want to go out to dinner now. Maybe we'd better stay here."

"Oh, no you don't," Madeline said, apprehensive about Gus's intentions and her own ability to resist them. "You still have a few dinners left to make up for that first picnic, remember?"

Gus looked at her in disbelief. "You're a hard woman, Madeline Mark. I can't believe you'd hold a grudge for so long."

"Who's saying I'm holding a grudge?" she

asked, hoping the lighthearted tone of her voice revealed nothing about her inner turmoil. It seemed like forever since she and Gus had been alone, really alone, and she was surprised at the intensity of her feelings. Maybe she should never have agreed even to a business date.

"I also seem to remember a lot of other nice things that happened that same evening," Gus pointed out, giving her an amused smile. He went over to an antique banjo and began to strum "By the Light of the Silvery Moon."

"Stop that!" Madeline said, more sharply than she'd intended. She didn't want to be reminded of that night. "This is a working dinner, remember?" She'd been so careful to keep her feelings back. Now that they were at the culmination of their professional endeavor, they couldn't revert to that beginning, beautiful as it had been.

"Okay," Gus said agreeably, walking over to the door. Madeline got her sleek black envelope bag and followed him. "Ready for some Vietnamese food?"

Madeline looked at him in surprise. "Vietnamese?" In answer to Gus's affirmative nod, she could only laugh. "I've lived all over the world, you know, and I've never had any Vietnamese food. I guess now is as good a time as any to start as any." She never knew what he'd come up with next.

"No time like the present," Gus agreed. "I can't help it if you had a privileged upbringing."

Later, as they pulled up in front of a tiny, unassuming restaurant, Madeline suddenly recognized the name. "Mai Que!" she exclaimed with delight. "That's where Thui works—Maurice's girl friend," she explained to the puzzled Gus. And then quickly she told him the whole story. "Maybe she'll be here tonight. I can talk to her, find out where Maurice is." Her eyes were alight with a new energy.

"Playing Cupid," Gus teased, opening the door for her. "Madeline Mark, matchmaker."

"No, no, that's not it at all," Madeline said, blushing slightly. "It's just that I'm worried about him. I've got to find him." They walked through the dimly lit restaurant and took a seat in one of the back booths, Madeline studying the waitresses with a keen interest.

"Well, in that case, I guess we'd better find out which one is Thui," Gus said. When a slight young woman brought them water and a menu, he asked her if she knew Thui.

"Oh, she's over there," their waitress replied without hesitation. She indicated a round table at the back of the room where an attractive woman was working with a stack of receipts.

Madeline and Gus looked at each other. "Let's order first," Madeline said, smiling at him. "Then if you don't mind, I'll go over and talk to her."

"There's nothing you do that I mind," Gus said, returning her smile. "Surely you know that by now."

To Madeline's relief, he didn't seem to expect an answer. Instead they both studied the menu, and after some discussion, ordered dinner. Then, having waited as long as her patience would allow, Madeline made her way to the round table at the back of the room.

"Thui?" she asked gently. The young woman

looked up, surprised. "I'm Madeline Mark. I work with Maurice."

The woman's eyes widened in recognition, and the faintest hint of a smile appeared on her lips. "Oh, yes, Maurice has spoken often about you." There was a regalness about the young Vietnamese woman, a delicate beauty that Madeline found irresistible, and almost immediately she was the girl's advocate, her champion. She was dressed simply in a blue cotton skirt and white blouse, but there was an elegance about her that couldn't be denied. Her long black hair was straight and shiny, flowing to her gently rounded shoulders, and her almond eyes were black. No wonder Maurice was so much in love.

"I'm looking for Maurice," Madeline said hastily, afraid she had been staring. "He hasn't been to rehearsal most of this week, and I'm worried about him. Do you have any idea where I can find him?"

Tears welled up in Thui's eyes and she shook her head. "I haven't seen him in more than a week," she said, her voice almost a whisper. "And I don't expect to hear from him again." At this, her voice found strength and she sat up a little straighter, as if the truth, hard as it was, had given her courage.

Madeline didn't want to be intrusive, but she needed to know what was happening. "His parents have laid down the law, haven't they?" Her voice was quiet but persistent as she tried to draw out the young woman.

Thui looked startled for a moment, her soft eyes misting over once again. "How did you know?" she asked, nodding affirmatively. The pain in her voice left nothing to hide.

Madeline sat down at the table beside Thui, covering her hand with her own, trying to comfort her. "I've heard rumors," she said simply. "And I'm sorry, very sorry. I wish there were something I could do."

"Oh, there is," the girl replied urgently. "You've got to find Maurice. Don't let him give up his music. He must never do that, never." The determination in her words almost stifled the sob in her throat.

"That's exactly what I hope to do," Madeline assured her sympathetically. "But what about you? What will you do?" She didn't know why she cared, but she did. Maybe it was her own unhappiness in love that made her sympathize with the anguish in Thui's face.

"I'll be all right. In Vietnam, these things are not unusual. Most marriages are still arranged by our families. I couldn't let him go against the wishes of his parents. I could never do that." Once again there was real courage in her words, courage and great devotion. "I'll be fine." She smiled slightly. "I've got my family here, my work."

Madeline didn't know what to say in the face of such poise, such conviction. After exchanging a few more words with the young Vietnamese, she excused herself, promising to keep in touch, to let her know what happened with Maurice. But it was hard to shake the sadness she felt, even when she was once again seated across from Gus.

"Did you find out anything?" he asked expectantly.

Madeline shook her head. "No, not really. She doesn't know where Maurice is, and she doesn't expect to see him again. They've broken up." She repeated all that the girl had told her.

"Life is cruel," he said ruefully. "Especially when we're not free of someone else's influence."

Madeline looked up at him sharply. He wasn't just talking about Maurice's troubles, she was sure of that. But she didn't pursue his line of thought, turning instead to her own dilemma. "He's got to turn up sooner or later. I wish there were some way I could help him."

"Something tells me you'll find a way," Gus declared, passing her a spring roll.

"I certainly intend to try," Madeline replied. Then, deciding it was time for a new subject, she added, "In the meantime, I'm going to enjoy this wonderful dinner. I'm absolutely starving." She took a sip of the Chinese beer Gus ordered. "How did you find this place anyway? You haven't even been in Houston as long as I have."

"Oh, I know some tricks." Gus laughed and then apparently decided to come clean. "I read about it in a magazine, then asked the people at the Plaza. They said it was great."

"Well, they were right," Madeline assured him. "It's just what I needed."

"A little meat on those bones," Gus said approvingly. "You've been working too hard, Markey. And it's not going to get any easier. The pressure is really on now, and I suppose you realize that."

This was the first mention either of them had made of the upcoming recording session. Madeline decided that they might as well talk about it and get it over with. "I know. I had a long talk with Brew about it this afternoon. I think we're ready. It's a little soon, but I think we'll be all right."

"All right?" Gus said in disbelief. "Today's rehearsal—what I heard of it—was absolutely amazing. The music's fine. It's the actual process that has me worried. It's a big change from the sort of performance the orchestra is used to—and you too, for that matter."

"Don't worry about me," Madeline returned confidently. "I can adjust. I never thought something was going to be difficult or impossible just because I hadn't done it before. I've recorded lots of live performances."

"But never a soundtrack," Gus insisted. The expression in his eyes was one of interest and concern. "It's different. You have to conduct while you're actually watching the film. So there's an added complication—you have to keep your eyes on the movie while you're conducting."

"I can do it," Madeline said confidently. "Besides, I've already seen the film, Gus. I love it. It's wonderful. The music can only make it better. And believe me, I'm looking forward to playing a part in making the movie the best it can be."

"I know that," Gus said patiently. "I just want to warn you not to get too impatient when we actually begin scoring the picture. It'll be different from anything you've ever done before. There are two types of scoring—"

Madeline interrupted him. "I know. We can use free timing, where I look at the film and conduct the orchestra, or we can use a click track, where you provide me with a beat and a time sequence you've already set up. Which did you have in mind?" She pronounced the phrases with a false sense of bravado, not wanting Gus to know that she'd gotten them out of a book on film making. The truth was, she was more nervous about this than she cared to admit.

Gus looked a bit surprised. "I thought we'd try it with free timing. If it's all right with you, I thought I'd arrange for the entire orchestra to see the film. That would give them an opportunity to imagine the way the music should work with what's already there." He paused, his expression a bit downcast. "If it doesn't work, we can always go to a click track." He looked up at her. "Of course, that seems to me to take away from the element of spontaneity —and I hate to think of you conducting the score with a set of headphones clicking out the rhythm in your ear."

Madeline had known that this was what was involved, but she didn't really want to think about it. She could do anything for Gus and his music, even something she'd never done before. "You just let me know what you think is best, Gus. I'm sure we can adapt. In the meantime, a screening for the musicians sounds like a great idea. I know the film is good because I've already seen it. Now they have to know it, too."

Gus reached across the table for her hand and held it tightly. "You're a real pro," he said with admiration. He seemed scarcely to have noticed his familiar gesture, as if holding hands with her were the most natural thing in the world.

"I know it." Madeline tried to be as casual as he seemed to be. "Don't worry about it. Just don't go getting all artistic and possessive about your music at the last minute, all right?" She was being flippant, hoping that her lighthearted tone of voice would cover her unease.

"Of course I won't, Markey," he promised, looking down at her hand in his. "You're the one I've always wanted for the job. You can do it." He lifted her hand to his lips and gently kissed her fingers.

"I know I can," she began, her heart racing wildly before he interrupted her.

"Besides," he said with a smile that lit the depths of his black eyes, "there's only one thing in my life that I think is worth being possessive about right now, and that's you. As soon as this soundtrack is behind us, I'm going to prove it to you—once and for all."

7

The excited babble on the sound stage sank to whispers as the lights dimmed and a blazing white spotlight appeared on the projection screen in front of the room. "This is a great idea!" Madeline heard Brew whisper as the movie began to roll.

She gave Gus a quick, sidelong glance. She could tell he was nervous. He had paced around outside until the projectionist told him they were ready to start, and then he raced in at the last minute, taking a seat next to her in the back of the room. It was obvious that he was anxious about the orchestra's reaction.

"Maybe this *wasn't* such a good idea," he murmured to Madeline. "I'm as nervous as a cat. Maybe it would be better if only you saw the movie."

"Don't be silly," Madeline said in a sharp whisper. "It's a beautiful movie—a great movie. Besides, you didn't make up the story. You only wrote the music. Remember?"

"I know." Gus sighed and looked over at her. "Hollywood nerves. I've been around this gang too long. I'm actually starting to think it's my picture."

"Shhh," Madeline warned him. "Don't you want the audience to be able to hear the story?"

Gus slumped obediently in his director's chair, as Madeline surveyed the faces around them.

When the movie began, she could tell that the orchestra members were willing to be caught up in it. The marvelous shots of the spaceport and the spaceships taking off into the stars were a beautiful counterpoint to the dirty work the main character was forced to do. Madeline could hear the theme of the modern music running through her head already. It was going to be wonderful.

Next to her, Gus reached over and took her hand. She noticed that he had pulled out a box of chocolate-covered mints and was absently munching away. "You're never without your junk food, are you?" she whispered.

"Never," he returned with a short laugh. "Besides, I need it now. I can't watch a movie without it."

"Pipe down back there," Brew said in a loud whisper. "You've already seen this movie. We haven't."

Gus gave him a friendly okay sign and leaned back in his chair. Madeline couldn't believe how nervous he was. She'd have thought he was long past that by now. Everyone loved the music—she did, the rest of the orchestra did and she knew that the producer and director of the movie did. It wasn't like him to be so edgy. Granted, he did have a lot of nervous energy, she'd noticed that about him from the very beginning. But somehow, she'd thought he'd be calmer under pressure. This was a whole new side of Gus Noble. See, Markey, she told herself, you can't count on anything, not even your own first impressions.

When he got up a few minutes later and left, she wasn't even surprised. The first time she'd seen *Forbidden Stars*, he'd done the same thing. She'd wondered that day if she'd somehow disappointed him in her reaction to the film, but when she went out to the hall to look for him after the screening, she found him sitting on the floor, a sheaf of music paper spread out in front of him. He was tinkering with the score, changing a note here, a note there. She was sure he was doing the same thing right now.

She waited as long as she could stand it. Then, seeing that everyone around her was completely engrossed in the film, she slipped out. Just as she'd suspected, he was out in the hall working. "What do you think you're doing?" she demanded. "No more last-minute changes. My musicians would revolt."

"Oh, come on, Markey," he said with a plea in his voice. "Don't you want to do everything you can to make the music perfect?"

"Right," she assured him. "I do, I really do. But there's a limit, you know. I can't keep giving the orchestra changes and expect them to turn in a perfect performance on the day of the recording. And you know that as well as I do. It's too much."

"Okay, okay." He slapped the papers together. "I get the point. But seriously, I do think that there are a few changes that might be good."

"All right," Madeline said with an air of resignation. "What are they?"

Gus shuffled the papers again and started showing her what he was doing. "See what I mean? Don't you think this would make the whole thing better?"

Quickly, she became caught up in the entire process, and as always, she loved working with Gus. Despite their disparate musical tastes, somehow they seemed to send off sparks that inspired each other's music. She had to admit that Gus's instincts about the changes were perfectly correct. Everything he thought of would improve the score, she knew that.

Their rapt concentration was broken by the sound of applause from within the screening room. Madeline and Gus both exchanged smiles and began to gather up the papers on the floor. "See, I told you they'd like it," she said with a smug grin.

"Markey," Gus said in a tone of mock disappointment. "I never thought you were the sort of woman who'd say, 'I told you so.'"

"Aha! He finally admits he doesn't know me as well as he thought he did." She laughed as she ducked past him through the swinging doors that led into the room.

The lights had come back on now and all of the members of the orchestra were standing around chatting excitedly. They all seemed impressed, and Madeline felt sure that now they would be even more eager to get to work on the actual recording.

And, she reflected, Gus had been right. It had made them feel special to have a screening just for themselves. The man really did have good instincts. Now if only he could keep calm through the recording sessions. If only *she* could, she thought nervously.

"All right, folks," she announced. "That's it for this evening. I want you to go back home and get a good night's sleep. We begin recording tomorrow morning. I'll see you back here at nine A.M."

There were a few grumbling sounds from the symphony members. Madeline knew that a few diehards would go out for a good time, but she noticed that all of the truly serious musicians, the ones she counted on, were getting ready to leave. She went to the door to tell everyone good night as they departed.

Maurice gave her a shy nod and a smile and went out first. He seemed a little more relaxed, she thought, but then with Maurice it was often hard to tell. When she'd seen him come in early at rehearsal that morning, she'd taken him aside for a personal talk.

As if he'd sensed what was coming, Maurice had been the first to speak, nervously pushing back an unruly lock of blond hair. "I know that I've missed rehearsals," he'd said, "but I have been practicing. I know that you could fire me if you wanted to, but I can assure you that there's a reason for all this."

Madeline had been touched by his distress, realizing once again how very young Maurice was, how much he had to learn. "I know there's a good reason, Maurice. I've met Thui." At his shocked expression, she had hurried on. "I have only two things to say. An unhappy love affair can hurt you—that I know from bitter experience—but it can also make you a better musician. Use your concern, your sadness—put it into your music. This isn't the time to run away from your talent, it's the time to throw yourself into it."

"Thank you," he'd said quietly, his expression chastened. "I won't miss any more rehearsals."

"I know you won't," Madeline had said encouragingly. "I know it's really none of my business, Maurice, but Thui is lovely. Sometimes true love is worth taking a chance on—even a big one. You have a promising career ahead of you, never doubt that. If you really love her, don't let anything stand in your way. It's simply not worth it."

"You're right," he'd said thoughtfully. He had stood up and headed for the door. "Thanks, Ms. Mark. I'll work it out."

She had sat back in her chair, glad that the encounter was over. Her eyes had caught their reflection in the mirror and held it for a moment, as she ruefully chastised herself. What a hypocrite she was! She certainly wasn't taking any chances. She knew that everything she had said to Maurice held true for her and Gus as well, but somehow it seemed easier to give advice to someone else instead of taking it herself. She wished she had more courage.

She looked across the room at Gus. They had spent a great deal of time together lately, and it had been almost torture for her. He had shown her the ropes of the sound stage, patiently answering her every question. Respecting her wishes, though, he hadn't once crossed the lines of their professional relationship. Sometimes the tension between them was so great it seemed unendurable, but somehow their commitment to music had prevailed—though Madeline had moments of wishing she weren't so sensible. She couldn't tear her eyes away from the corner where he was standing and talking to some of the studio people.

She thought she would never get used to the surprise of seeing him. he had been the last thing she'd expected in her life, the last sort of man she thought she'd ever be interested in. Tonight, he had on white corduroy jeans and running shoes and a navy blue turtleneck, casual and elegant all at once. Her lips parted with a fond smile as she watched his impassioned conversation.

Her reverie was broken by a voice at her side. "I can't wait!" T.R. was standing there, clanging imaginary cymbals. "I'm so excited I don't know if I'll be able to sleep tonight. I love it."

"Oh, you'll be able to sleep," Madeline assured him. "You'd better. I'll work you so hard tomorrow, you'll drop in your tracks if you don't."

"Oh, all right," T.R. grumbled. "I can't wait to go home and tell my teenagers about this. They're certainly going to be impressed." He gave her a smile and sauntered out the door.

"Now there's a man who likes his work," Gus said dryly, walking up to her. The room was deserted, only a few stragglers out in the hall. The studio crew was beginning to rearrange the chairs in preparation for the recording session tomorrow. Gus looked around one last time. "Guess we'd better go."

"Right." Madeline tucked her purse under her

arm and began to lead him to the door, waiting while he gathered up his papers. "I'd better get some sleep."

"I'll walk you to your car," he said matter-of-factly. She was a little surprised that he didn't attempt to prolong the evening, hurt and relieved at the same time.

They walked through the parking lot, breathing in the clear November air. Madeline felt her blood race, and she knew it wasn't just the cooler weather. It was the sense of possibility that Gus always evoked in her, the idea of being out with him in the night, under the stars.

"I don't suppose we need to work tonight," he said hopefully when they reached her car door. They had spent several evenings over the past week working together, and Madeline had enjoyed the companionship. Being with him had given her a sense of security; it was something to look forward to at the end of the day.

"I don't think so," she replied quietly. "Tomorrow we'll find out if we've worked hard enough." She wanted to ask him over for a drink or coffee, but she knew what that could lead to. Her emotions were running high tonight—she felt excitement at seeing the film again and the musicians' favorable response to it, and also worry over the recording session. It would simply be too easy to lose her fragile control.

"I wish we could be together, Markey," Gus said, brushing her cheek with his hand. "Especially tonight."

The slight touch made her quiver, and for a moment she almost relented. She wanted to be with him, more than anything else in the whole world, but she knew it would be a terrible mistake. She needed to rest and to think, and most of all, to be alone. Tomorrow was going to be an important day and she wanted to have all of her energies firmly focused. She had to keep her distance right now, just as she had been doing, or tomorrow would be a disaster for all of them.

"It wouldn't work, Gus," Madeline said reluctantly.

Gus pushed his glasses back on top of his head impatiently, and when he spoke, his low voice was filled with anger. "You can't hide from me forever, Markey. Once this is over, we're going to be together again. Just because you have some crazy notion that we can't work together and love each other at the same time, you're punishing both of us. We have a lot of unfinished business, you and I, and don't think you can put it off forever."

She was too honest not to acknowledge the truth of his words. "You're right," she said, reaching for the handle of the car door. "We do have unfinished business. But this isn't the time or the place to take care of it. We'll have other nights besides this one."

"We'd better," Gus said fiercely and, completely ignoring the rules of their agreement, he gathered her up in his arms. "We'd just better." He leaned down to kiss her and Madeline couldn't resist. The evening spent in such close proximity had made her want him terribly. It seemed silly to deny herself this single pleasure when she was denying so much more. She knew that this kiss would only intensify the longing, but that would have to be enough—for tonight.

Her lips had parted for his kiss, and when his tongue reached the interior of her mouth, she began to weaken, pressing her body close to his, giving in to his demanding embrace. She knew that it would be difficult to withdraw after this, but she so much wanted the reassurance of his body next to hers that she let it happen, heedless of the consequences.

"I have to go," she whispered as she drew back, still within the circle of his arms.

"Don't!" The word was more a command than a request, but Madeline knew Gus was only feeling the same need she did.

"I have to," she insisted, freeing herself and opening the car door. "See you tomorrow, Gus. Bright and early." Her heart ached to leave him standing there alone.

He didn't respond, only stood there shaking his head as she got into the car and drove away. Madeline kept glancing at him in her rearview mirror until she was about to turn the corner out of the parking lot. Then he turned and headed for the building.

The drive back to her apartment seemed to take forever, and when she finally reached her home, it seemed empty and lonely. She had thought that she would work for a little while, but instead she went straight to bed, where she tossed and turned for most of the night. Finally she drifted off just before dawn, to a sleep filled with restless dreams of Gus's music, a constant echo of her newfound loneliness.

Madeline got up early the next morning, determined to put her dreams behind her and get on with things. This is going to be a good day, she thought to herself. This is all going to go well. I just know it. But there was still some lingering doubt in her mind, and she found that she was nervous about seeing Gus again.

When she walked into the studio and saw him talking with a group of people near the control booth, her heart leapt. Maybe she had been foolish, she thought. Maybe Gus was right, maybe she was punishing them both. When he saw her come in, he walked over immediately.

"Sleep well, princess?" he asked with a wicked smile. "I didn't."

"Neither did I," Madeline admitted, thinking of her dreams. She looked up at Gus in silent appeal. Don't push me, she thought. Not now. Not when we both have so much at stake.

She was conscious of his gaze as she looked around the room. The chairs and music stands were all arranged, and microphones were everywhere, with long strands of connecting cables running across the floor. The sound booth was filled with machines and people moving in and out of the small, cramped space. Madeline felt a momentary panic at her lack of control. Gus seemed to sense it, for he didn't press her, only took her arm and led her into the booth.

"Madeline Mark, meet Adam James, the sound engineer, in charge of overall quality." Madeline shook his hand gracefully, liking him on sight. "And this is Jenny Laker, the mixer." The young blond woman smiled up at Madeline.

"Looks like the orchestra's ready to get started." Gus gestured toward the chairs, which were almost filled.

Madeline saw that almost everyone had arrived and was busy tuning up. The musicians were eyeing the microphones on the music stands suspiciously. Last night, caught up in the spell of *Forbidden Stars,* this had seemed like a glamorous, exciting place. This morning, in the cold, harsh studio light, some of them looked a little bemused, as if they were uncertain how to proceed.

"If you'll excuse me, Ms. Mark," Adam said, "I think I'd better start checking sound levels. We want this to go as smoothly as possible from the start. Saves time and money for all of us."

Madeline was grateful for his professionalism, and she nodded her approval as Adam set about his business. Madeline felt thrown by the complicated dials and gauges, though she had recorded music before, and she was glad that Adam seemed so competent. Jenny was helping him and Madeline didn't want to be in the way, so she stepped out of the booth, with Gus right behind her.

He put his hands on her shoulders possessively, and his black eyes stared into hers. "Okay, Markey," he said in a low, urgent voice. "Why don't you go out there and warm up? Don't let me down."

"I won't," she promised, hoping that she wouldn't. For the first time, she felt uneasy about playing Gus's music in front of this audience. What audience? she asked herself sharply. That was part of the problem. That was the big difference. The musicians would be playing only for Gus and for the people who were part of the studio staff. Perhaps that's why everything seemed so different.

She tried to put aside her feelings of unease as she took her place in front of the orchestra. She gave a reassuring smile to let them know that she had confidence in them. "Good morning!" she said cheerily.

They returned the greeting as if they were a single voice.

"We are about to begin what may be one of our most interesting experiences together. Not really begin, of course, for we have been working toward this moment for a long time. Let's do it as well as we always have in rehearsal. Are there any questions about the changes Mr. Noble has made?" She glanced around, seeing most of the musicians shaking their heads, looking at her with respectful attention. "Then let us begin."

She waited for the projectionist to roll the film up to the very beginning of the movie, then raised her arms majestically, leading the orchestra into the star theme for the opening shots of spaceships traveling through the galaxies. So far, so good. The orchestra seemed to be inspired. They were straining, reaching for the glorious high note that was the climax of the theme, then suddenly—

"Sorry! Sorry!" Adam James was shouting and coming toward them. "This mike isn't working properly. Let me see what I can do with it." He walked over to the mike attached to Fig's music stand and started fiddling with it.

Madeline was so shocked that she realized it must have been almost a full minute before she lowered her arms to her sides. Everything had been going along so beautifully that the interruption seemed like a bad dream. Not a good omen, she told herself wryly, as she watched the orchestra members grumbling among themselves. Fig sat there in silence, his rapidly moving eyebrows the only evidence of his displeasure.

She tried to be patient, though she had assumed that the microphone had already been checked. Even so, she knew that innumerable problems could occur during recording. She looked around at Gus, who shrugged his shoulders before turning to say something to Jenny Laker. No help there.

Adam apologized and went back to the control booth. The projectionist rewound the film, and they began again. The second try went even better than the first. They had completed the star theme and were moving into the modern second movement, the driving, pulsing music, when again—

"Hold it!" Adam used the microphone in the control booth this time, and the interruption took everyone by surprise. "You're two beats off the projection, Ms. Mark," he said matter-of-factly. "Let's try to pick up the tempo."

Madeline clenched her fist. In her judgment, she was exactly where she should be. She looked over at Gus, who only shrugged his shoulders. When everyone was ready, she took a deep breath and began again.

Little did she know that the pattern for the entire morning had been set. Stop and start. Stop and start. It was absolutely maddening. Madeline was used to playing something all the way through and playing it well. She tried to control her mounting fury, knowing that it was hard enough on the musicians already without adding her personal fuel to the fire. She'd just have to get through this as best she could.

"Lunch!" she called finally, after what must have been the fifteenth interruption. "See you back here in an hour."

The musicians put down their instruments in relief and headed out of the room en masse, most of them giving Madeline only sidelong glances. Somehow, she felt as though she'd failed them, as though this whole dreadful morning had been her fault. But she knew it wasn't. She walked over to a chair in the corner and sank into it with a sigh. This really wasn't going at all well.

"Hey Markey, have a drink!" Gus appeared at her side, carrying, miraculously enough, a glass of iced soda water with lime. She accepted it gratefully. "How're you doing?"

She looked at him skeptically. "How does it look like I'm doing?"

"Okay," Gus said, though Madeline wondered if she could detect any doubt in his voice. "Relax. It's just a different setting for you, that's all. You'll get used to it."

"Never," she swore softly. "I will never do anything like this again. Usually, I only have to worry about music critics after the performance. Here"—she gestured toward the control booth— "everyone's a critic. And they can stop us right in the middle of anything—as if they have no respect whatsoever for the difficulties of making music."

"Now who's getting temperamental?" Gus asked with a trace of irony. "These people are just doing their jobs. And they're good at them."

"Meaning I'm not?" Madeline looked directly up at him.

Gus rocked back and forth on the balls of his feet and shook his head at her. "I don't mean that at all. Besides, we could always go to a click track. That might make it easier."

"Great! Then instead of Adam yelling at us all the time, I can hear a metronome beat in my headphones." She put her glass down on the floor beside her chair and stood up. "You don't think I can do this, do you?" she demanded angrily.

"I know you can do it," Gus replied calmly. "I just want you to do it in a way that gets the job done and makes us both happy. And I know from bitter experience that it's hard to score a film the way we're doing it."

"I'm sure you do," Madeline said shortly. "I'm sure whoever conducted the score for *Prince of the Rodeo* didn't have these sorts of problems."

"That's right, I didn't," Gus said evenly.

Madeline just stared at him in amazement. "Then why aren't you doing it now?"

"I don't want to and I don't need to," Gus said firmly. "You're the best. It's natural to use the Metropolitan Symphony Orchestra when the film is being done here, and I'm lucky that you're a part of it. That's your orchestra out there, remember? They're going to respond to you much better than they would to me."

What he was saying was perfectly reasonable, and she was pleased by his faith in her, but she still was worried about the afternoon's work. What if she couldn't get it right? What if this session went on forever—stop and start, stop and start? She didn't think she could stand it. For the first time in her life, she doubted herself, and it was the most frightening thing she'd ever experienced.

She looked across the room at some of the orchestra members who were returning from lunch, and wondered if she looked as tired as they did. It had been a long morning for all of them. Catching her eye, Adam gave her a friendly wave from the control booth. "Well, Gus," she said in a determined voice. "Let's get this show on the road." She breathed a silent prayer that things would get better.

Like the morning, the afternoon was marred by constant interruptions. Madeline, her concentration broken time and time again, thought she was doing her best, but apparently it wasn't good enough.

Adam kept marking the beat, stopping the performance when they got out of sync with the film. Even Gus broke in occasionally with suggestions and criticism. By four o'clock, her nerves were in shreds, and from the looks of it, the musicians weren't feeling much better.

"Let's take it again, folks," Gus said, after going over a few notes with the string section. "And this time, let's get it right." He looked up at Markey expectantly, saw the expression on her face, and looked at his watch as if it were suddenly the most interesting thing in the world. "No, it's late. Let's pick up again tomorrow."

"See you all in the morning," Madeline said, trying to smile, trying to ignore the anger and dismay she felt rising within her. "You did good work today." She wanted to reassure the musicians, hoping they understood that she knew how difficult this was for all of them. As quickly as she could, she gathered up her papers and headed for a small office to the side of the sound stage, hoping to be alone for a few minutes.

Gus came in and shut the door behind him. "I didn't mean that the way it sounded, Markey," he said apologetically. "As a matter of fact, I've heard you say it yourself in rehearsal. 'Do it until you get it right.' I'm sorry if I was out of line."

"Well, you were," Madeline pointed out sharply, her exhaustion rising in a furious flash. "I don't know how anyone's expected to work under these sorts of conditions. I'm tired, the musicians are tired and the composer's saying 'one more time.' It's been a long day, Gus." She reached for her briefcase, turning to face him.

"I know how you feel, Markey," Gus hurried to reassure her. "It's always this way. The technology is intimidating, there's no audience—everything is different for you, but—"

His placating tone only irritated her further. "If you think you can do any better," she said in a calm, clear voice, "do it yourself." She turned and left the room, her head held high, fighting hard to keep her feelings under control.

An hour later, she was pacing around her office, thinking about the situation. She'd been unfair to Gus, she knew that—she'd simply made him a victim of her own frustration and self-doubt, taking one remark and blowing it all out of proportion. She would do this and do it well. She was a conductor, she reminded herself, one of the best, and tomorrow she'd perform like one. A flash of white caught her eye, and she looked up to see a white handkerchief, tied to the tip of her baton, waving in the doorway. Madeline stopped her pacing. She had a pretty good idea who was behind the white flag.

"May I come in?" a familiar voice asked hesitantly. Then the white flag and voice were followed by Gus, who slowly stuck his head in through the open door. "King's X?" he ventured, his black eyes contrite.

Madeline couldn't help being a little relieved. She had behaved abominably, and she knew it. "Come on in, Gus," she said, sinking wearily into the chair behind her desk. "That is, if you're still speaking to me."

Gus peered at her over his glasses. "I might ask you the same thing, you know." He was still holding the white flag up over his head.

"I spoke first," Madeline snapped back petulantly. Then, immediately sorry for her snide remark, she relented slightly. "Oh, put that thing down," she said with a sigh. "I don't need any reminders of what just happened." She looked up at him, her eyes meeting his directly for the first time since she stormed out of the recording studio.

Gus took the white handkerchief off the baton, stuffed it in his back pocket and handed the baton to Madeline. "I've never seen you throw a temper tantrum before," he admitted.

Madeline looked thoughtfully at him for a moment. Then a slow smile crossed her face. "That's what it was, wasn't it?"

Gus nodded solemnly. "That's what it was, all right," he confirmed. "A real-life, bona fide temper tantrum."

Madeline had the good grace to look embarrassed. "I've never done anything like that, not in my whole career." She leaned forward earnestly, her arms folded on the desk, her gray eyes wide with disbelief. "I'm sorry, Gus. I don't know what got into me. But it wasn't fair of me to take it out on you."

"It was a rough day and a big job," Gus said sympathetically, his eyes never leaving her face.

"It's not my first rough day," Madeline said disconsolately. "And I've had other big jobs. I apologize for letting you down." That was one of the things that was bothering her most about this job: She was afraid that the intense feelings she had for Gus were putting her under additional pressure.

"You haven't let me down," Gus insisted, putting both hands down on the desk in front of him and leaning forward, "as long as you'll be back tomorrow."

"Oh, I'll be there," Madeline promised, "but you really don't need me." She got up and started walking around the room. "You could probably do this better than I can. I'm sure the taping for *Prince of the Rodeo* went much more smoothly than this one." She was still feeling a little petulant at not having known about that.

"Are you kidding?" Gus's black eyes were wide with disbelief. "I went home every night and ranted and raved to the four walls. I thought I'd never get it right, and I was afraid I might drive the studio orchestra crazy trying to. You were a peach today compared to the temperamental fool I was."

Madeline laughed at the image of Gus ranting and raving. Even if it wasn't true—and she had no reason to think it wasn't—she knew that he was telling her about it to show her he knew how she felt. For the first time, she felt she could share her doubts.

"I may not be the best person for this," she replied, shaking her head. "This is your music. You know it better than anyone else. You know how it sounds in your head, how it goes with the film. I can't compete with that."

Gus walked over to her and put his hands on her shoulders. "I'm not asking you to compete with me. Everything you say is true—except for one minor detail. You know this orchestra inside out, better than anyone else, and they respect you. Of course, if you were a little more familiar with the movie, it would help tremendously."

His words had given her back her faith in herself, but she couldn't keep from asking one more time, "Do you really think I can do it?"

"Surely you have more confidence than that, Markey. You're one of the finest conductors in the country. And you know that as well as I do." He was standing across the room from her now, his black eyes flashing indignantly.

Madeline couldn't argue with that and she knew it. "Of course I can do it. It's just that I—"

Gus didn't give her time to finish. "Now you're talking," he said excitedly. "Now you're sounding like the Madeline Mark I fell in love with." And as he moved across the room toward her his eyes said more than his words.

Madeline could scarcely believe what she was hearing. She looked up at Gus, her eyes locked in his affectionate gaze. When he gathered her up in his arms, she knew there was nothing she needed to say or do, nothing except allow herself to be caught up in his enthusiasm.

Secure in his arms, she finally whispered, "Thanks for believing in me."

"Oh, Markey, Markey," Gus answered, "don't you know there's nothing you can't do?" He pulled back slightly and looked down at her, his eyes filled with unabashed longing. "Don't you know how much I care?"

Madeline smiled back. "Yes, I guess I do." And then she gave herself up to his kiss, tender at first, then passionate and fierce, the fire they had been holding back rising to the surface, more forceful than ever.

When Gus finally released her, Madeline felt both weak and strong at the same time—weak from the relentless power of her own sensual feelings, strong in the knowledge that she and Gus had something real and viable, something lasting. And she knew she had a job to do. "Do you think you could arrange for me to see *Forbidden Stars* again tonight? Maybe twice?"

Gus grinned. "It's already set up."

Madeline was taken aback. "How did you know I'd say yes? I might have thrown you out of here bodily!"

Gus shook his head. "No, you wouldn't. I knew you wouldn't quit." He kissed her tenderly on the lips. "One of these days, Madeline Mark, you're going to have to admit that I know you better than you think."

"Oh, you do, do you?" Madeline pinched his nose playfully.

"You better believe it," he answered quietly. "And I've just started. Before I'm through, I'm going to know you inside out. You just wait and see."

She didn't doubt that he meant what he said, and she felt a thrill of pleasure as they left the office, hand in hand. All her uncertainty was gone, replaced by her joy at Gus's confidence in her. They were all right again, and that was all that really mattered.

8

The red velvet curtain parted a second and third time as the gala Christmas crowd demanded more. The applause and the number of curtain calls were proof that the opening night of the traditional *Nutcracker* Suite had been a complete success. On the fourth curtain call, Madeline returned to center stage, bowing formally to the delighted audience at Jones Hall, her face glowing with a triumphant flush. As usual, she was beautiful in a black tuxedo, her black hair twisted in braids, the elegant pearls mixed this time with mistletoe in honor of the Yuletide season.

With a flourish of her hand, she had the orchestra stand, a section at a time, for another bow, and the audience acknowledged each group with enthusiastic applause. When they were finally done, Madeline blew a kiss to the crowd and one to the orchestra, then departed the stage for the last time. She was immediately greeted backstage by friends and well-wishers who eagerly gathered around her.

"Thank you, thank you very much," she said, shaking hands with first one, then another. She always enjoyed these immediate few moments after a performance. The enthusiasm of all those behind the curtain was infectious and she loved being caught up in the excitement. But tonight was different, for her heart was divided. She was looking for more than applause tonight. She was looking for Gus. The look in his eyes would be all the applause she wanted.

As she graciously made her way through the crowd, Madeline searched the sea of faces for his familiar black eyes, his tousled shock of black hair, his impetuous smile. At every turn, she expected to see him, taller than anyone else, waving at her from across the room. When she didn't spot him, she had to fight back a surge of disappointment. He said he'd be here, and for the last few weeks, they'd been almost inseparable. It wasn't like him not to keep his word.

She was soon swept up in a wave of holiday greetings. The musicians were all still full of the energy that comes with a good performance, and the holiday spirit seemed to have affected the members of the board who'd attended that evening. Mamie and Brew kept her busy for a few minutes, but finally Madeline managed to escape to her dressing room for a few solitary moments, still wondering where Gus was.

"Markey, are you all right?" Angel's voice was concerned as she knocked on the door.

"Sure, come in." Madeline turned her attention to the dressing table and began gathering up her makeup and putting it in her purse. She adjusted the small sprig of mistletoe in her hair. "Merry Christmas! The holiday spirit is certainly in the air tonight."

"That's what I thought too," Angel replied a bit shyly. "I was wondering if you'd like to go out for a drink with us later—you and Gus, I mean. I can't believe he's not here. Is anything wrong?"

"Nothing at all," Markey replied brightly. "I'm sure he just got held up somewhere. He'll be along. But I think we'd like to take a rain check on the drink, if that's all right." She wanted to wait for Gus but she didn't want company.

"Sure thing—see you later." Angel gave her a quick smile and hurried out the door.

Madeline smiled at her retreating friend. Everyone who knew her had seemed to accept that she and Gus were involved. It should be pretty obvious to them by now, she thought, remembering the last few weeks. She and Gus had worked closely together to finish the soundtrack, and she realized how foolish she'd been, how much time she'd wasted, simply by being afraid of the relationship, afraid of sharing her life with him. Now that the recording was finished and Gus was doing the post-production work with the technicians, she missed seeing him during the day, surprised at the void it had left in her life. But, determined to make up for lost time, they had spent every evening they could together, and she knew she had fallen in love.

She smiled at the thought of it—being in love with Gus. With patience and gentle prodding, he had gotten past all the barriers she'd erected within herself to find the woman underneath. She'd told him all about the affair with Martin Singer, her fears about the new job, her dream of finding a home in Houston at last. In turn, he'd told her about the actress he'd lived with for two years in Malibu who'd left him for a director, his brief stint as the manager of a rock and roll band, his eventual breakthrough into the movies. Their relationship had been so easy and so natural that Markey wondered at herself. Why had she made it so difficult? What had she been so afraid of? And through the period of discovery, the music that they shared brought them even closer together. For the first time, she had gone back to playing the piano—duets, in fact. Gus even encouraged her to start composing again. Her life had suddenly become complete.

When someone knocked on the door, she raced across the room and threw it open. It was getting so late it had to be Gus, but to her surprise, it was only Brew. She tried to make her voice welcoming as she asked him in.

"I'm sorry I'm not Gus, Markey," he said with a grin, "but that's why I'm here. He called the office just now, asked me to tell you that he was sorry he missed the performance, and he'll see you at home. He was awfully apologetic." He sat down in the chair she offered him.

"Was anything wrong?" she asked quickly, but Brew only shook his head.

"He sounded fine," the older man reassured her. "Maybe a little rushed. You two getting along all right?"

"Yes, we are," Madeline said with a proud smile. She chuckled inwardly at how far she had come—why had she been so worried about being so discreet? It didn't seem to matter to anyone, except Mamie, and now even she seemed to think of the two of them as a couple. "I'm surprised he didn't make it tonight. Something must have come up."

"That happens," Brew said noncommittally. "I want to tell you something though, Markey—you're doing everything right. The soundtrack brought in lots of money, and season ticket sales have been consistently high. You've been magic ever since the day you hit town and don't think the board hasn't noticed. The tour will be the icing on the cake. I've been charged with the pleasure of telling you, though it's a little early for Christmas, that you've got a home with this orchestra for as long as you want it. I thought you and Gus might like to celebrate." He sat back in his chair and pulled out his pipe.

Impulsively, Madeline leaned over and kissed him on the cheek. "Thank you for telling me, Brew. It's what I always wanted." She paused, as if considering the news. "Houston has been so good to me," she confessed, tears coming to her eyes. "I've had such good luck here. It's a wonderful orchestra; everyone's been so pleasant to work with, and—"

Smoke filled the air as Brew chuckled. "Not to mention meeting Gus Noble." He put his pipe back in his mouth and stood up. "So what are you waiting for, maestro? Plan to stick around here all night while he's cooling his heels? Come on, I'll walk you to your car." He opened the door and Madeline followed him out, grateful for his humorous understanding.

She had to be careful driving home that night. She wanted to speed a little, to hurry to Gus and tell him her wonderful news. Passing a pay phone at a convenience store, she almost stopped, then realized that that would only add a few minutes to the trip. She wanted to see him, wanted to hold him in her arms again. There simply had to be a bottle of champagne in her apartment somewhere, she thought. Tonight was a night to celebrate, and Gus was the person she wanted to share it with.

Madeline thought that she owed much of her success to Gus and his love. It wasn't the soundtrack recording, though that was a professional challenge she was glad she had met with Gus's help. He had changed her, just by being himself, by being a part of her life. Their shared joy had enabled her to be more expressive, more open to all of life's experiences, not just her music. It was a debt she could never repay.

She hurried into her apartment building, acknowledging the security guard's pleasant greeting with a friendly smile. The Checker cab had been parked out front so she knew Gus was waiting, and for once, the short elevator ride seemed interminable. She turned her key in the lock and was surprised to find that there were no lights on in the living room. She stepped in cautiously and turned on a table lamp. She knew Gus was here, because she could hear his voice. There, she thought, listening for a moment, he's in the bedroom.

She stood in the doorway for a second, not wanting to interrupt him, but not wanting to eavesdrop either. He sat on the huge bed's white satin spread, talking into the white phone, his voice angry and frustrated. "I'm telling you I'll do what I can, Evan. I'll get back to you as soon as I can. Now I've really got to go." He slammed the receiver into the cradle and sat staring at the phone.

"Gus, what's wrong?" Madeline asked, taking it all in. He'd planned to go to the symphony, that much was clear. His black evening jacket was thrown across the bed, and the black tie around the neck of his tuxedo shirt was untied.

"Oh, Markey, I'm sorry," he said sadly, then turned around, as if he were looking for something. "I meant to come, I really did." He got up and came toward her, his hands behind his back. He leaned forward to give her a quick kiss, then pulled out a small, artful bouquet of white violets. "I realize it's not the same as being there to give them to you after the performance, but here they are—a little wilted, I'm afraid," he added glumly. "Can you ever forgive me?"

Madeline took the flowers and inhaled their sweet fragrance. "Of course I can. Tonight wasn't the only performance. I was a little worried, that's all. Is everything all right?" She'd never seen him look so distraught. He usually seemed so calm and in control. This simply wasn't the Gus she knew so well. "Come on, tell me. What's the matter?"

He gave her a crooked smile, his black eyes

rueful as they held hers. "Nothing. Everything's great—too great in fact. The last soundtrack I did has just been nominated for an Academy Award and one of my songs is up for a Grammy. Evan— that's my agent—said that half the calls he's gotten last week have been job offers for me. He tried to track me down at the Plaza for the last week, and I finally returned his call tonight. I never dreamed I'd be on the phone so long." He gestured to a legal pad next to the phone, filled with notes of names and phone numbers. "I'm sorry I missed you tonight—but we have the rest of the evening. We could still go out to dinner, if you like."

"Oh, no you don't," Madeline teased him. "You think going out to dinner will get you off the hook. Not true, Gus. I'm going to make you stay right here until you've apologized to my satisfaction." She slipped the tie from around his neck and began to unfasten his shirt studs. She leaned forward to kiss the base of his throat, savoring the racing pulse she felt there.

"I could apologize like this forever," Gus murmured, drawing her close. "I may have to miss more of your shows, if this is the way you're going to react."

"Not on your life," Madeline said boldly, backing him up against the edge of the bed, then giving him a gentle push. She stretched out along the familiar length of his body, enjoying the sensation of power.

This was what she could never get over—the way making love with Gus seemed new and different every time. It was as if he had enabled her to rediscover her sensual nature, the side of her life she'd neglected since her unhappy affair. Gus delighted in her body, never seeming to get enough of her, always wanting more. It was a sweet victory she'd won, she thought, when she curled up next to him under the satin sheets.

"Now tell me again how much you missed me," she demanded, as his mouth sought first one breast, then the other, coaxing her into arousal.

He laughed, his breath against her skin more sensual than any music she could imagine. "Maybe you should be telling me that," he returned, and she obliged, reaching for him.

The sweet lovemaking was a welcome release from tension and both of them seemed to realize it, quickly taking their pleasure, but tempering their desperate need with moments of affection. Madeline had never realized how much she could need Gus, need his touch and his intimate caresses. He had encouraged her to be passionate, to experiment, and her trust had led her to give herself completely. Afterwards, as they lay side by side in each other's arms, she stroked his black curls, then let her hands slide slowly down his body to hold him close in a fierce hug. She couldn't believe she had ever been afraid of this relationship; it had brought her more pleasure than anything in her life, even her music.

"So how was your day?" Gus teased lightly, his voice against her shoulder. "Aside from missing me, I mean. How was the performance tonight?"

She laughed at the double entendre. "The performance right here was worth a standing ovation." She grinned mischievously. "And the orchestra wasn't bad either." She lightly pushed him aside and got out of bed, going to the closet and taking out a lavender robe. "But man cannot live by love alone. I'm going to fix us some dinner."

"I'll help," Gus offered, reaching for a pair of jeans hanging over the chair. "Be right there."

She hurried off to the kitchen, feeling slightly wicked, surprised by her own thoughts. They'd have a light snack, some champagne to celebrate their good news, and then they'd make love again. It was that sort of night, she thought, but then every night with Gus was like that. "How about pizza and champagne?" she suggested, as Gus came into the kitchen. "It seems that's all we have."

Gus stood there and looked at her with astonishment. "Madeline Mark, I never thought I'd see the day when you were ready to eat pizza voluntarily!"

She pulled the pizza out of the freezer and popped it into the oven, then handed him the champagne. "You've been a bad influence on me," she teased. "I'll be buying popcorn and candy bars before you know it." She reached into the cabinet for two long-stemmed glasses. "Watch it!" she cautioned as the cork sailed across the kitchen.

Gus filled the two glasses and handed her one. "To us!" he said, reaching forward to wrap his arm around her, then holding the glass to his lips.

"To your awards," Madeline returned. "I hope you win them all." She wanted him to know how pleased she was by his recognition. Then she gave a satisfied smile, thinking about the future. "To Paris!"

She held her glass to her lips and drank deeply. Gus had promised to meet her in Paris for a week while the orchestra was on tour, and for the first time, she found that she was genuinely looking forward to the trip. But when she looked up to see Gus still holding his glass, not drinking, she was frightened. "What's the matter?"

"Markey, I can't come to Paris now." He put his glass down on the table and put his hands on her shoulders. "I have to go back to California—tomorrow, in fact. Evan said that there were so many offers waiting for me that I needed to decide —and fast—which ones I wanted to accept. I've already lost a week. I need to go back there, line up my next commissions, and then I'll be back. I can't come to Paris. I'm sorry." His eyes were sad as he searched her face for her reaction.

"I see." Her voice was tight and controlled, and she hated herself for it. "You're leaving tomorrow and you're not coming to Paris." All her old fears rose to the surface. He was leaving. He wouldn't be back. She should have known this would happen sooner or later.

"But I'll be back," Gus insisted. "You know that I can work anywhere. But first I have to line up my commitments. After I meet with Evan, I'll know where I stand, then I can pick and choose. I'll be back before you know it." He tried to pull her close to him, but she backed away.

She pretended to be busy, checking the pizza, then taking it out of the oven and putting it on plates. Handing one to Gus, she took a seat at the table, then held out her glass. "More champagne," she demanded, and Gus filled her glass, a puzzled look on his face. "To your work," she offered ironically. "It brought us together and now it's taking us apart. I hope it makes you happy, Gus. Happier than I've made you."

Gus put down the slice of pizza that he was holding and stood up. He walked over to the refrigerator and leaned against it, his own anger barely controlled. He seemed to be choosing his words carefully. When he spoke again, his voice was almost calm, but dangerously quiet. "You're not being fair, Markey. You should be happy for me. I never expected this sort of reaction. Where's your faith in me? I told you I'd be back."

"Of course you did," she said spitefully. "But when?" She knew she was acting crazy, but she couldn't seem to stop herself. She knew Gus meant what he said, she knew that he cared, but she was frightened. She'd been left before and she didn't want to experience that again. It had been too painful. Now that she had grown to love Gus, to trust him, she couldn't believe he was going to disappear.

"As soon as I can," he promised. He came back and took a seat at the table, reaching for her hand. "By the time you get back from Europe, I'll be back here in Houston. It shouldn't take me more than a couple of weeks to get things squared away out there." He stroked her fingers, his touch sure and gentle, as if he were trying to convince her by his caress. "What are you so worried about?"

"I don't know," she said tiredly, but when she thought about it, she realized what was really bothering her. "It's just that I thought tonight would be so lovely, that we could celebrate our news, and that things would just go on and on."

"What's your news, Markey?" Gus asked softly. "You haven't told me."

It didn't seem to matter now. "Brew said that I

have a home here as long as I want it. The orchestra is doing so well that the board is pleased with everything—the soundtrack, the tour, everything. I'm going to stay here, Gus. It's what I've always wanted." But would she be happy, she thought, would it be the same without Gus?

"Honey, that's wonderful," he said, holding her hand to his lips for a kiss. "I'm so happy for you." His eyes not meeting hers, he added, "I wish you could be happy for me too."

"I am," she said dully. "I want you to have the recognition you deserve. You're a wonderful composer, Gus," she went on, her voice warming slightly. "It's time everyone knew that."

"Then why are you acting this way?" As if his patience had run out, Gus dropped her hand, and leaned back in his chair, his voice sharp. "You knew all along that *Forbidden Stars* was coming to an end, that I'd have to find some other project to work on."

"But we never talked about it." As soon as she said the words, she realized why.

"You never asked. You never seemed to care what I'd do next. Damn it, I love you, Markey, but you haven't asked. I've always been concerned about your work, but you haven't really asked about mine." She knew that the anger in his voice was justified, and she felt ashamed that Gus had given her more than she had given him.

"I know, Gus," she admitted. "It's not that I don't care, it's just that I've been afraid. I knew this moment would come sooner or later. And tonight, just as I was feeling that life was safe and secure, that I could begin to settle down here and put down roots, I find out you're leaving. It's like my whole world is falling apart."

"Oh, come on, Markey," Gus's voice snapped. "Grow up. I told you I'd be back, and you have to believe in me. It's only for two months at the most, and part of that time you'll be in Europe on tour. What did you expect me to do, twiddle my thumbs here while you went off with the orchestra? I have to work too, you know. And you have to trust me. When I say I'll be back you have to believe me. Is that asking so much?"

She knew she was being unreasonable, but her fear had gotten the best of her. "Not really, Gus. You're right, I know you are. It's just frightening to me to think about your not being here."

"But I'll be back." He got up and stormed off into the bedroom, then came back and tossed a small blue velvet box across the table. "Here. Here's some proof."

Madeline opened the box, half-joyfully, half-sadly, knowing what she would find inside. A large diamond solitaire winked up at her brightly, and her eyes filled with tears. "It's lovely, Gus."

"Then take it. And wear it. Wear it all over Europe, wear it every day. It's a promise I'm making to you." His voice held no anger now, only stern conviction. "The oldest promise in the world."

"I can't." She looked up at him sadly, then snapped the box shut. "It's too soon. We haven't really been together that long, and now we're going to be apart for a while. It simply wouldn't feel right." This wasn't the time to make such a commitment, she thought—or was it? She shook her head, pushing the box back toward the center of the table. It was late and she was tired and drained. The night that she'd thought would be so special had gone all wrong and she wasn't sure how to make it right. Oh, she could take the ring, she knew that, but she also knew that Gus had to go back to California to see what his life there held for him. It would be better to wait. "We have to be sure," she told him finally.

"Damn it, I am sure!" he insisted. "You're the one who's holding back out of some adolescent fear of being abandoned. Let it go, Markey, before it's too late. You're not just going on a tour, you're on a detour—from life, from the real world. From me." He stormed into the bedroom.

She followed, watching with despair as he gathered up his things and whirled to face her, his keys in his hand. "If you decide to start living, you know where to find me," he said harshly, heading for the front door.

As he slammed it behind him, she went over to the sofa and sank onto it, drawing her knees up to her chest and wrapping her arms around them. She felt very lonely and ashamed. Maybe Gus was right. She was afraid to take chances. Did that mean she was afraid to start living? Maybe that was better than being hurt, but maybe not. She only knew that she'd never been so unhappy in her entire life. The elegant apartment seemed empty and cold without him. Was that what her life was going to be like?

Her eyes fell on the box wrapped in silver paper on the coffee table—Gus's Christmas present, the score of *Forbidden Stars*. She'd had it bound for him in fine black leather with a silver quarter note embossed on the cover, and now he'd left without it, without even knowing about it. With tears streaming down her cheeks, she took the box and put it on the shelf. Maybe that's where it belongs, she thought, a closed book on a shelf, an unopened present. She went off to the bedroom, knowing that she would have to give in to her grief. What had she done? What had she lost?

9

Bonjour!" The voice of the chambermaid was bright and cheery as she entered Madeline's room, pulled back the curtains to let in the sunlight and deposited a tray of hot chocolate and croissants on a table.

Madeline roused herself—had the night really gone by that quickly? For that matter, had the tour really gone that quickly? She pulled on a fluffy, warm wraparound bathrobe and walked over to the window, looking out at the cold winter sunlight. Paris! It was all stretched out before her as if waiting for her to come out and play.

Nice to have a day off, she thought, attempting to feel more cheerful at the prospect. In reality she dreaded the time to herself, where before she would only have welcomed it. Too much time on the road, she reminded herself ruefully. Too many hotels, too many meals in restaurants, too many rehearsals in strange places.

Still it had been a success, she had to admit that. The critics had raved about the symphony and about Madeline herself. Many of their performances had been greeted by standing ovations. It had been successful beyond her wildest dreams. Even the first performance, in Athens, had gone virtually without a hitch; and it was the most special one for her, for that was where her parents were living now. The brief reunion with Henry and Julia Mark had given her a lot to think about. Forty years and they were still happy together. It was something to be proud of.

"Are you happy, Markey?" her mother had asked. "I know you're doing well professionally. The music says it all—and I'm always reading about you in the papers and magazines." She raised a hand in admonition as if knowing what her daughter was going to say next. "And I know you write when you can. But you never tell us much about your life beyond music. Sometimes I think I ruined your life when I made you take piano lessons."

"Now stop that!" Madeline laughed. "That's what you say every time I see you, and while that's not very often, you ought to stop worrying about it. I love my work. I love my music."

"But do you love anything else?" Julia Mark was not a woman to let a line of inquiry drop.

"I don't know," Markey confided impulsively. "There is someone. . . ." And almost before she realized it, the whole story of her relationship with Gus Noble had tumbled out. "But I tried to make things right," she added. "I called him at his hotel in

Houston, but he'd already checked out. Right before I left, I called him at his number in California and only got his answering machine, but I left a message."

Julia gave her daughter a sympathetic smile. "What did you say, Markey?"

Madeline had the grace to blush slightly, but she knew she wanted to be completely honest with her mother. "I told him I wasn't afraid anymore—that I was ready to start living. I don't know if he got the message or if he even cared by that point. I just don't know where it will lead," she concluded with a sigh.

"It sounds as if it's leading somewhere," her mother said, laughing. "Just follow it. See where it takes you."

"I'm not in a position to be following anything right now," Madeline said with a touch of finality, "except for the itinerary of the tour." She looked at her mother speculatively and decided the moment was right to ask the question she had always wanted to ask. "You followed Dad all over the world, Mother. And to do that, you gave up a promising career as a concert pianist, I know. I still have all the reviews of your early performances. I found them in a box in the attic of our house in London and I've kept them with me ever since. Don't you have any regrets?"

"So that's where those papers went," her mother said. "I wondered."

Madeline wasn't about to let her off the hook so easily. "Any regrets, Mother?" she insisted.

Julia Mark gave a beatific smile that was legendary in diplomatic circles. "None at all, Markey.

None at all. I would have followed your father to the ends of the earth—and there were times when I thought I had. But I wouldn't have changed a thing. And I still play. Granted, I don't play for applause, but then, that was never really important to me. If I had been a different person, if we had lived in different times, I might have tried to have my career and my marriage. I don't think I wanted the career enough, that's all. But now most women seem to be having both. Who knows? Maybe you'll be one of the lucky ones. I hope so."

"I hope so too," Madeline said fervently. She didn't even care about marriage at this point. She only hoped that she could have Gus and her music. The talk with her mother had eased things for her somehow, and she realized how much she missed her parents. This time in Athens had been precious to all of them. Even her father, usually such a reserved man, had told Madeline time and time again how proud they were of her. Henry Mark hadn't pushed for information about his daughter's life, but then he never had.

But that was Athens and this was Paris, Madeline mused as she looked out the window. That was then and this is now. She dressed and got ready to go out when she heard a knock on the door. "Mademoiselle Mark?" called a questioning voice. "C'est Jean Pierre."

Madeline recognized the voice of the concierge of the small French hotel and hurried to open the door. At first, she couldn't even see his face for the flowers! They were everywhere—a wild mélange of daisies, roses, orchids and carnations that seemed to include every color of the rainbow. "These are for you." Jean Pierre smiled. "Just came this morning." He walked over to a small table and put them down, handing her the card.

"*Merci,*" Madeline said with a smile as she reached into her purse for a tip, clutching the card in one hand. She waited until Jean Pierre had left before opening the small white envelope. She knew who it was from. The message was short and to the point. "I wish I were there with you, but then I suppose you know that. Love, Gus."

She laughed. She'd been wondering when the flowers would arrive. It had begun in Athens. When she returned from a day's shopping with her mother, she'd found her room filled with flowers. Under her mother's curious gaze, Madeline had opened the card, which read, "Got your message—and it was the best news I've had in my life. You've only been there a week, but it seems like forever. Hurry home. Love, Gus."

Her mother, to her great relief, hadn't asked any questions. She only smiled as if she knew all she needed to know.

Madeline had thought that the gesture was perfect, Gus at his best. She was glad that he seemed to have understood her apology. Her own fears and doubts had caused her such pain, and she knew that she could only make it up to him in person.

From time to time, she reminded herself that she had as much to give Gus as he had to give her. She had been selfish and uncaring, so wrapped up in her own world, her own problems, that she'd forgotten to share his. He had had a life before she met him, a life filled with good work and important commitments; a life she had, to her shame, largely ignored. In the future, she would make sure that didn't happen again. There was really nothing to be afraid of.

Pleased as she'd been by that first gesture, she hadn't expected anything more, so she was surprised when the flowers arrived in Rome. "Stay away from those Italian men. I suggest a tour of the Vatican. Love, Gus." He had sent more to Vienna. "Don't go waltzing without me." And one rainy, cold day in Amsterdam, she had returned from rehearsal to find her room ablaze with color. "Can't wait to kiss your tulips again. Love, Gus."

And now, here they were in Paris. The flowers were in her room and Gus was on her mind. Paris was the next-to-the-last stop. One week here, then a week in London, then back to Houston. It had all been better than she'd expected, especially after she'd heard from Gus. And the members of the symphony had enjoyed the tour as much as she had.

Even Maurice seemed to be relaxing a bit, Madeline reflected. His performances had been brilliant thus far, and he would be a featured soloist at the performance in London. She had thought that through carefully and finally decided that he deserved the chance. Throughout the tour, it was as if the young flutist had undergone a remarkable transformation from a reserved, unhappy man to a talent and personality of great charm. Madeline wondered if Thui was responsible, if Maurice had made some sort of decision, but she was reluctant to press him about it. As long as he was doing his job, that was all that mattered. Besides, she thought ruefully, you're a fine one to be offering advice to anyone. Look what a mess you almost made of your life.

She dressed and went down to the hotel lobby, determined to enjoy her last day in Paris. The flowers from Gus had gotten her day off to a good start, though they were a bittersweet reminder of the last day Madeline had seen him. What did it matter if they were together in Paris? What mattered was that they might be together forever. She checked the hotel desk for messages, and when she turned to go out, Angel was standing near the door, looking at a guidebook. "Markey," the young woman said brightly, "feel like some company?"

"Sure," Madeline returned eagerly. "What did you have in mind?" She would welcome the distraction, she thought, for it would keep her from thinking too much about Gus, about what might have been. And her friendship with Angel was easy and comfortable now. Besides, the girl looked like she could use some company.

"I'd like to see the Tuileries," Angel suggested, "but it's a gray day for gardens, isn't it? I'd really like to see everything, but there's so little time. I wish I knew my way around better."

"You've found the best tour guide you could possibly have," Madeline declared. "I lived in Paris with my parents and I studied at the Sorbonne. Angel, I'm going to show you things no tourist has ever seen."

She was as good as her word. Throughout the

day, she led Angel through a merry chase of museums, galleries, dress shops and landmarks, until they finally collapsed in a small café on the Left Bank.

"You weren't kidding, were you?" Angel laughed. "You really do know everything about Paris!" She looked at her shopping bags with pleasure. "I ought to know, I feel like I've bought half of the city by now."

"It looks that way." Madeline gave the shopping bags an amused glance. "I enjoyed our day too, Angel. It really took my mind off things."

"You mean Gus Noble," Angel said perceptively. "Everyone knows there was something special going on with you two and somehow it went wrong at Christmas." She looked sympathetic.

"It was all my fault," Madeline confided impulsively. "I made it go wrong. I was so selfish, so wrapped up in my own life, that I wasn't really sharing things in his life. He was supposed to come to Paris, but then he couldn't, and I flew off the handle. Bad timing, I guess. He had to go back to California and see about some new commissions, and I felt deserted, afraid he'd never come back." She felt better for having shared her problem. It was the sort of thing she hadn't done enough of, and she knew she had to make a start somewhere.

"Are you kidding?" Angel looked shocked. "With the way he looks at you? I remember when we were recording *Forbidden Stars*. The man couldn't take his eyes off you. He'll be back, Markey. Don't doubt it. Besides, if things work out for you, you'll have to get used to it. Look at me

and Jim—here I am and he's back in Houston."
She paused, as if thinking she'd said too much.
"You have to trust him, Markey. And trust yourself.
You two seemed so happy together."

"We were," Madeline admitted. She went on to
tell Angel about that first night at the drive-in movie
with Gus. "That was fun."

Angel shook her head and laughed. "Of course it
was. That's what you need, Markey. All work and
no play . . ."

"Speaking of work." Madeline looked at her
watch. "We'd better get going. Drink up. We're
going to have to take a taxi back to the hotel, and
even then we're going to have to rush to get ready
for tonight."

Angel gasped when she saw the time, hastily
downed her Campari and soda and gathered up
her packages. "Don't worry, we'll make it," she
reassured Madeline. "You haven't missed a performance yet. Besides, they can't start without
you."

The two women enjoyed the ride back to the
hotel, talking about the places they'd been and the
things they'd seen. When Madeline went to her
room to dress for the evening's performance, she
was more relaxed than she'd been in ages. The day
with Angel had helped and she was grateful for the
young woman's friendship. She knew how to give
of herself, and Madeline knew that was a lesson she
still had to learn. But she was trying very hard. She
wished she could call Gus, tell him she was ready to
pick up where they'd left off. She wanted to
apologize for being so childish. She was a grown

woman and she'd found her man, the one she wanted to spend the rest of her life with, if he'd still have her. She looked longingly at the phone but knew she had to talk to him in person. This was not a message she dared trust to long distance. She wanted to be able to touch him, to hold him, to show him as well as tell him. That was the only way. The bedside clock showed that her time was running out. She'd have to hurry to make the performance. Rushing out the door, she knew somehow that her apology would keep until she got home.

The performance went very well, and Madeline was glad she'd chosen a piece that was as flashy and exciting as Beethoven's Ninth. Though it had required intense rehearsals with members of the Paris Opera, it had been worth it. She knew she would always remember it as a high point of the tour, and that the symphony members, quite rightly, would always be proud of that performance. The standing ovation said it all.

Everyone was in a celebratory mood that night when they went to dinner after the performance. They were a relatively boisterous crowd in the elegant French restaurant, and Madeline was glad to see that spirits were so high. The champagne flowed freely as they had their dinner, and Fig and T.R. entertained them with stories of other tours with other orchestras. Even Madeline joined in, telling tales about Wolf Trap and the all-important summer season there. Before she knew it, the dinner was over, and they were drinking fine cognac and nibbling at *crème brûlée*.

"I propose a toast," Maurice said a bit self-consciously, as he rose at the other end of the table from Madeline. He held his brandy snifter in her direction. "To Markey—the wonderful conductor who has made this all possible!"

The other members of the party rose and toasted her. Madeline was so moved she could hardly speak, and it meant even more to her that the idea had originated with Maurice. He had changed somehow and she wished she knew the reason.

She soon found out. Figaro, with a wicked grin, raised his glass high. "And to Maurice Spender. To a good performance in London, and to an even better one on his wedding night, which is not too far away!" Everyone laughed and cheered and started showering Maurice with questions.

Figaro leaned over and whispered in her ear. "He just got a letter from Thui today. He asked her to marry him before we left, but she wanted some time to think—I'm glad she didn't take too long. And things are going to be all right with his family too. Once Maurice told them he didn't care what they thought, they came around pretty fast, not wanting to lose their only son. Things do have a way of working out." He sat back in his chair, sipping his brandy, wiggling his eyebrows up and down expressively.

Madeline laughed and went around to offer Maurice her congratulations. "I'm glad it worked out," she said, leaning down to kiss him on the cheek, smiling when she saw him blush at the unexpected gesture.

"If it hadn't been for you, it might not have," the young man returned quickly. "Thank you, Markey.

You were right about everything." He dipped his head a little shyly. "Thank you for caring so much. And Thui thanks you too."

Madeline went back to her seat, delighted that things had turned out so well for Maurice and Thui. The party brought back the bitter memory of her last evening with Gus, an evening that could have been as wonderful as this one if only she'd let it. He seemed so far away now, though the flowers in her room let her know she was in his thoughts. She hoped he knew how much she was thinking about him.

After the celebration, she went back to her room and packed for the trip to London early the next morning. One more stop. One more week. Would Gus be in Houston when she got there? What if he'd changed his mind and gone back to California?

She looked longingly at the phone and thought about calling him to thank him for the flowers. It would be an extravagant gesture, she thought. But after calculating the time, she thought it would probably be a mistake. And what if he wasn't there? She couldn't leave another message on the answering machine. No, this was something she'd have to wait and straighten out face-to-face.

The time in London went by more quickly than she had anticipated though, and it was an anticlimax after the pleasures of Paris. The second night there, they performed Mozart's Concerto for Flute and Orchestra in D Major. It was a fluffy little piece, and Madeline thought it would add some wit to their program for the evening. She also thought that it would give Maurice the opportunity he had deserved for a long time. Sure enough, Maurice performed brilliantly, and when the reviews came out in the London papers, the critics sang his praises. Madeline couldn't have been happier for him. And she was happy for herself as well, for the only problem she'd had with a member had practically resolved itself.

The tour had been another challenge in her life, she reflected, as she packed her bags for the trip back to the States. She had always hoped that someday she would be a famous conductor, revisiting the places in Europe where she'd lived with her family, where she'd gotten her musical education. And now she'd done it.

So what next? She leaned back on the suitcase, pressing it shut. That was the question. She had to see Gus, had to talk to him, make him see that she had learned from her mistake. And if he offered her the ring again, she was going to take it and put it on her finger forever. She had been so foolish. She could see that Angel and even Maurice knew the facts of love, truths she'd ignored for too long.

She realized with a start that she hadn't heard from him the whole week in London. She'd come to count on the flowers, to wait for them. Maybe she should have called him. Maybe he'd finally given up on her. No, she thought firmly, he'd be there for her. She simply had to trust him and have faith in her own feelings.

Resolving to put these thoughts out of her mind, she went into the dressing room of her hotel suite to get ready for the final performance of the tour. As a change from her usual feminine version of a tuxedo, she chose a long, black velvet dress that hugged her slender body. For some reason, she wanted to feel frilly and feminine tonight. It was almost medieval, with full loose sleeves that gave her an easy range of movements, and a full skirt below the fitted bodice. Trimmed with heavy silver braid, it made her look both authoritative and elegant.

She had just picked up her baton case and evening bag and was ready to leave when there was a knock on the door. Thinking it might be Angel wanting to share a cab to the performance hall, she dashed to get it. But when she opened the door, it was only the bellman bearing a long, slim white box. "For me?" she asked joyfully, accepting the box, and giving the bellman a large tip that would be the talk of the hotel for days.

She waited until the man had quietly closed the door behind him before opening the box. On a bed of white tissue paper lay a single, perfect red rose. Madeline's eyes filled with tears—she knew what it meant. The card was pure Gus. "You've been gone so long I'm not sure I'll recognize you, but if you'll wear this when you get off the plane, I'll make an effort to pick you out of the crowd. HURRY. Love, Gus."

Oh, she would hurry home. The rose was all she needed to turn her heart in that direction. He would be waiting for her, just as he said he would. She would never worry about her feelings for him again. She'd already kept him waiting too long.

Gently reaching out to touch a velvety petal, she knew Gus was making a promise, a promise he would keep. She realized with a thrill of pleasure that she had promises of her own to keep, promises she'd waited too long to make. She was ready for the rest of her life to begin.

10

Hoping to catch a glimpse of Houston, Madeline pressed her nose against the cold window of the powerful plane, but it was too soon. Nothing was visible beneath the swirling layer of white clouds. With a frustrated sigh, she leaned back in her seat, closed her eyes and pressed her lips together impatiently.

No matter how hard she tried, she could think of only one thing—and that was Gus Noble. In the past month, she had come to know how important he was to her. Without him, everything else had a hollow ring. What good were triumphs half a world away when there was no one to come home to? And now that she was almost home, some of her old doubts were beginning to return. What if he wasn't there? Maybe she should have phoned.

Maybe she was foolish not to have called him from every country. What if it was too late? Her palms were damp from anticipation. It would be all right. It just had to be, she told herself, trying to sound reassuring. But what if it wasn't?

Madeline turned her head slightly, opened her eyes and saw her reflection in the small window beside her. She was glad she'd chosen her new black Chanel suit. Its lightweight wool had withstood the trip nicely, and the ruffles on her white silk blouse added a feminine touch to the otherwise severe tailoring. Her hair was pulled back in an attractive and practical French knot, and Madeline knew she looked as good now as she had when she'd boarded the plane in London. She wanted to be beautiful for Gus.

I *have* been afraid of living, she told herself ruefully, thinking back to that terrible fight at her apartment. She had been so angry, so unyielding, so inconsiderate of his needs. She was going to have to make it up to him, no matter what it took. And she was ready to start as soon as she got off the plane, provided he was there to meet her.

"What's the matter, Markey?" Angel inquired gently from her seat beside Madeline. The two women had enjoyed each other's company during the long flight, but now that they were getting close to Houston, Madeline had withdrawn into her own thoughts. "You haven't been the same—aren't you glad to be going home?" There was genuine concern in Angel's voice.

Madeline looked over at her companion, trying to manage a smile. "I'm sorry, Angel. I didn't know it was that obvious. Of course I'm glad to be going home. It seems like we've been gone forever."

"I know what you mean," Angel replied, an understanding look in her blue eyes. She poked at the ice in her plastic glass. "I'll be glad to see Jim again. I'm even looking forward to hearing his bad jokes." She smiled wistfully and took a last sip of her soft drink.

"You're lucky, Angel," Madeline remarked, with a longing smile of her own. "Jim's a good man. I like him a lot." But she was thinking about Gus, wishing she could be as certain of him as Angel was of Jim.

The young woman seemed to be reading Madeline's mind. "He's going to be there," she said, her eyes filled with compassion. "I just know he will."

Madeline looked at her friend and smiled. They both knew Angel was talking about Gus. "Well, he said he would be—but you never know." She looked out the window, knowing that she sounded ridiculously pessimistic and wondered if she was trying to ward off bad luck by thinking the worst.

"I suppose that's why you've carried that single red rose all the way from London," Angel quipped heartlessly. She indicated the solitary flower stuck in the back pocket of the seat in front of Madeline.

"Okay, so I'm being silly," Madeline conceded with a self-conscious laugh. "But you don't know him like I do, Angel. He's the most unpredictable man I've ever known." Even as she said that she knew it was an exaggeration.

Angel shook her head in disagreement. "Well, he hasn't been unpredictable lately, you'll have to admit—flowers in every port sure as the sun sets in the west. T.R.'s been making book on it. The flowers in England cost him some money, though. They were a day later than he figured."

Madeline looked at Angel with wide eyes. "You're kidding me, aren't you, Angel?" She covered her mouth with one hand, trying to suppress an astonished giggle. "Tell me you're kidding."

"I wish I could, but you know T.R." She shrugged her shoulders helplessly. "If it hadn't been the flowers, it would have been something else."

"I don't believe it," Madeline said, as much to herself as to Angel. She was looking out the window pensively, her mind mulling over the incident. "How did you know who they were from?" She hadn't mentioned the flowers to anyone, and though she didn't think it was much of a secret, she was surprised that the musicians seemed to know all about them.

Angel gave her a reproving look. "Are you kidding? It's not real hard to figure out, you know. Every time you hear his name mentioned, you sort of blossom. Which is nothing compared to the way he looks at you. He's so much in love with you, it hurts just to watch him. I never—"

Madeline was spared the rest of Angel's explanation for, just at that moment, the pilot spoke over the intercom. They would be landing in Houston soon. The weather was moderate, no rain in the forecast. "Guess that means it's time for seat belts," Madeline said wryly.

"And not a moment too soon," Angel returned, looking pleased at the prospect of being home.

For the next several minutes, they were all occupied with the business of landing. The stewardesses were moving up and down the aisles, collecting empty glasses, checking seat belts, putting up pillows and blankets. Madeline's attention was on the ground below, her eyes searching for familiar landmarks—the Astrodome, the ship channel, Hermann Park—but Intercontinental Airport was on the outskirts of town, too far away from the part of Houston Madeline knew.

She sighed again, turning from the window and gathering up her belongings. When she had her purse and leather carryall ready, she took the red rose from its place in front of her. It was beginning to droop a little, but the fragrance was still sweet. She was sniffing the beautiful flower when Angel spoke again.

"You know, Markey," she said in a confidential tone, "everyone in the orchestra really likes Gus. As a matter of fact, we're all hoping you two will get married." She said the last words so fast that she was fairly breathless when she finished.

"Oh, Angel," Madeline replied with genuine emotion, "you've been a real friend to me on this trip, and it's meant a lot. I've never really had anyone I could talk to so easily." She leaned over and gave Angel an affectionate hug. "But don't you think you're jumping to some fairly broad conclusions? I mean, I don't know that you're going to lose me to anyone. I mean, well, you know what I mean." It all seemed so complicated that she gave up. The plane had started its descent now, and the noise was making it hard to talk.

But Angel wasn't through. She shook her head

177

solemnly. "Are you saying we don't know what we're talking about?" she challenged, gesturing to the other passengers on the plane. "One hundred musicians can't all be wrong."

Madeline laughed in response. The landing gear was just touching the ground, and it was impossible to talk above the noise of the engines. She turned to look out the window at the airport buildings coming into view. It was five-thirty in the afternoon, Houston time, and the late afternoon sun fell in shadows across the runway. But the sky was blue and the air clear. All in all, it looked like a perfect homecoming.

When the plane reached the terminal and stopped, the musicians let out a cheer. They were all glad to be home, to have the long trip behind them. Madeline sat in her seat for a few minutes, waiting for the others to go first. Now that the moment had come, she wanted to prolong it as much as possible. Besides, she wanted a chance to speak to the musicians before they dispersed.

"Come on," Angel said as she stood up. "Let's go." She had her purse over her shoulder and, in one hand, a large straw basket filled with books and souvenirs.

"You go on," Madeline said, with a wave of her hand as she too stood up. "I'll catch up with you." Then, for the next several minutes, she talked with the others. They would be taking a short break after the tour, and she wanted to express her pride in their achievement one more time.

When the last musician filed by, she turned to pick up her hand luggage. Catching a glimpse of her reflection in the window, she impulsively tucked the red rose in the crease of her French knot. Knowing she couldn't put it off any longer, she shouldered her carryall and headed up the aisle herself.

When she stepped out of the plane's door, she was met by the sound of applause. Standing on the top step, she saw that an enormous Welcome Home banner was being held in place by a crowd of well-wishers and fans. Surprised, she waved to the crowd, then began moving gracefully down the steep steps. She should have known there would be some sort of homecoming celebration but she hadn't given much thought to this part of the trip. But of course Brew had—and so had Mamie Spencer.

When she reached the ground, Madeline was immediately surrounded by friends and fans, each wanting to say hello first. For the next several minutes she gave herself up to the crowd, all hope of meeting Gus gone for the moment.

"Welcome home, Madam Conductor," Brew said, taking her carryall from her hand. "How was your trip? Everything went according to plan, I presume."

"It was flawless," Madeline assured him. "Your preparations were letter perfect. We had a great time—as you well know."

Mamie was on her right side by then. "The reviews have been wonderful. You were a smash success!" She was fairly bursting with pride.

"Well, not me alone," Madeline reminded the happy patron. "We were all in this together." She indicated the other musicians who were by this time caught up in their own private reunions, painful reminders of her own loneliness.

"Oh, but of course," Mamie continued. "Everyone was great, the papers all made that clear. But you were the apple of the critics' eyes."

"You'd better watch out, Mamie." With a wink at Madeline, Brew issued a mock warning. "We won't be able to live with her once she's read all those reviews. Better not show her the one in the *New York Times*."

Madeline was all ears now. "What did the *New York Times* say?" She knew they had been well received everywhere they went but she didn't know what the papers had written in this country, or that they'd written anything at all.

"I don't think we should let her read it yet," Brew teased. "Do you, Mamie? At least wait until we get her signature on the next contract."

Mamie was beginning to catch on. "You know, Brew, you may have a point there." But she squeezed Madeline's hand to show that she was only kidding.

Madeline was scarcely aware of their good-natured ribbing. She was searching the crowd, her gray eyes looking for a certain pair of glasses, a tall, black-eyed man. At every turn, she expected to see his smile, hear his deep musical voice. But she couldn't find him anywhere, and her heart sank as she realized he wasn't on hand to meet her.

Fortunately, she was caught up in the rush of the crowd. There was really nothing for her to do except follow the group out to the front of the airport where a chartered bus was waiting to take the musicians back to their cars at Jones Hall. She did her best to make small talk with those around her, to say thank you, it was great. She needed all the poise and self-assurance she could muster because she was just coming to terms with her disappointment at not seeing Gus there. She had been foolish. She had counted on it too much. Now she had to put on a good face for the people who were her friends. They were there to congratulate her. She couldn't let them down.

A black limousine waited in front of the chartered bus and, in spite of Madeline's protests that she wanted to ride with the musicians, Mamie whisked the beautiful conductor away, depositing her in the cool interior of the luxurious car. In spite of herself, Madeline sank gratefully into the soft depths of the back seat, relieved to escape the eyes of the crowd. She smiled politely at the driver, who merely touched his hat and nodded. Mamie was right behind her, then Brew, once he was satisfied that everyone who needed a ride was on the bus.

"Well, that's that," he said, pleased at having finished his duties. "We're coming into the home stretch."

"We couldn't have done it without you, Brew," Madeline offered sincerely, hoping that her voice betrayed none of the pain she was feeling.

"That's the truth," Mamie concurred brightly. "And the board will hear that from me, you can count on that," she assured them both. "Now—enough work for one day. I've got supper planned at home and I want you both to come over. I want to hear all about this trip, firsthand. And I want to hear it *before* anyone else."

Madeline didn't know what to say. She had counted on meeting Gus at the airport and didn't have any other plans. The last thing she wanted was to spend the evening making small talk, though she knew it would probably be better than being alone. "That sounds lovely, but—" she began.

"No buts about it," Mamie interrupted. "I know you're tired but I won't keep you long, I promise. Besides—you couldn't have possibly had anything decent to eat in the last fourteen hours. I know how those airline meals are." As they talked, the driver was starting to pull away from the curb.

Knowing when to give in gracefully, Madeline was about to accept the dinner invitation when, out of the corner of her eye, she saw the red Checker cab pull up behind the bus. Her heart leaped at its familiar sight. So he had come after all!

"Stop!" she cried. "That's my ride," she said, knowing that she couldn't pause to explain this to Mamie.

The driver did as he was told, though he didn't look too happy about it. "What's going on?" Mamie demanded in surprise.

"I'll have to explain later," Madeline began apologetically. "I don't have time now." She grabbed her purse and carryall and started to open the door. Thinking better of it, she stopped and turned back to Mamie and Brew. "Thanks," she said. "Thanks for everything." There was no time to say anything else.

Brew had obviously spotted the red Checker cab and had some idea of what was going on for he was grinning from ear to ear. "Don't worry, Markey. I'll take care of everything," he promised, indicating Mamie with his eyes.

Madeline blew him a grateful kiss and flew out of the car. As she shut the door, she could hear Mamie exclaim indignantly, "What was that all about?"

But Brew's soothing voice followed immediately. "Supper sounds like a fine idea, Mamie. You and I can have a nice long talk."

Madeline knew that Brew would make it all right for her. She was so excited at seeing Gus that she gave no thought to anything else. She didn't care what anyone thought, what anyone said. Her priorities were well fixed—nothing mattered except that she be with Gus again. But when she saw him get out of the car, his arms full of red roses, she stopped running. Her eyes met his and she knew there was no need to hurry. It was going to be all right.

"Markey!" he called out a little breathlessly. "You're back!"

Madeline put both her hands on her hips. "Right —I'm back and you weren't here. You missed the show." She had said this to him before, the night of the *Nutcracker*.

Gus gave her a rueful grin as he walked closer. He knew she was referring to their last argument. "Do you want to start again from the top?"

Madeline's heart sang out. The magic was still there. "You bet," she said, trying to act as normal as possible.

"Do you have any idea how hard it is to find roses in January—especially a lot of them? I didn't think just one would do it," he continued, moving toward her.

She laughed. It was so good to hear his voice, to know that everything was all right. They could work this out, she was sure of it. By the time she reached him, she had tears in her eyes, tears of relief. She gathered the roses in her arms and inhaled their sweet fragrance, giving Gus an appreciative glance. Then she dropped them on the hood of the red car and reached for him.

Suddenly, a cheer went up from the musicians on the bus beside them. Madeline had completely forgotten about the orchestra. As far as she was concerned, she and Gus were off in a world of their own. "We've got an audience," she whispered, looking up at Gus.

"I've never known you when you didn't, Markey," he teased. "I'm afraid it's one of those things I've got to get used to."

"Hey, Markey," Angel called out from the open door of the bus, "what'd I tell you?"

Madeline waved at her and laughed. "One hundred musicians can't be wrong!"

"Right," Angel said, nodding happily.

T.R.'s voice floated above the clamor on the bus. "Okay, you guys, time to pay up." He was walking down the center aisle of the bus, collecting money from his fellow musicians. "A bet's a bet."

"What's that all about?" Gus asked Madeline, a puzzled look on his face.

"I'll tell you about it later," Madeline promised, thinking how many other things she had to tell him. "It's a long story."

"I've got all the time in the world." He smiled down at her, his eyes filled with tenderness. Without saying another word, he gathered her up in his arms and, as if they were all alone in the world, he kissed her.

The musicians yelled for an encore and were delighted when Madeline and Gus paid no attention to them. Finally, the bus started rolling toward the street. Madeline and Gus stopped long enough to wave good-bye.

In the sudden silence after their departure, Madeline didn't know where to begin. "I tried to call you before I left. I couldn't find you anywhere."

Gus put his arm around her and they stepped back up on the sidewalk. "I had to get off by myself," Gus explained. "I thought I'd botched things for good."

Madeline stopped beside the red car, looking at him sadly. "That's what I thought. I was terrible that night, just terrible. Can you ever forgive me?"

"For what?" Gus asked, his arms encircling her waist. "For being afraid? For feeling vulnerable? I don't have to forgive you for that. I should have been more sympathetic, more definite. It's not as though you hadn't told me about your bad experience with that Singer fellow. I just wasn't listening, I guess." He leaned over and kissed her on the lips. "Besides, I was being fairly muleheaded."

"Well, now that you put it that way," Madeline said, rolling her eyes, flirting with him. Then she reached up and put her arms around his neck. "We need to talk. I have so many things I want to tell you."

Gus grinned. "Didn't anyone ever tell you that you can do a lot of talking without words?" As if to prove his point, he brushed her lips with his. The kiss began gently, then changed to something else, something fierce and unrelenting—a welcome reminder of their shared love.

Madeline responded with her whole heart, knowing that the time for holding back had long passed. She had already given Gus her heart and she wanted to show it in everything she did. When a passing driver honked his horn, she pulled away reluctantly. "What we need is some privacy."

"Well, this isn't much, but it will have to do." Gus held open the car door for her, waited until she slid across to the middle, then slipped in beside her. "This is private enough for what I have to say." He reached into his pocket and pulled out a familiar blue velvet box. "Ready to wear this now?" he asked softly.

"How did you get this?" she asked, surprised, remembering that she'd left it in the apartment.

"I kept the key you gave me," he said, his expression smug. "See, I told you I was coming back. And the key did come in handy. I stopped by your apartment to pick this up—pretty good reason for being late, wouldn't you say?"

"The best," Madeline said, holding out her hand. "And yes, I'm ready to wear it. I'm ready to start living, Gus. I want to be with you always. I'm never going to be afraid again." She rejoiced in the delicate caress of his hand as he slipped the ring on her finger. She held out her hand for his inspection, both of them admiring the twinkling diamond which caught the rays of the sun.

The ring was a reminder of a promise she had made to herself about Gus, a promise she intended to start keeping right away. "How long can you stay?" she asked eagerly. "Did your trip go well?"

She wanted him to know that she'd changed, that she genuinely cared about his work, his life, his needs.

Gus stretched his arm out along the back of the seat, his fingers reaching to touch her shoulders gently. "Pretty well," he said airily. Then his tone changed to one of unabashed pride. "Great! I have so much work lined up that I'll be busy for as long as I want to be. And I can do it all right here—with you. But it's not so much work that I can't take time out for a honeymoon." His black eyes were mischievous as he reached for her. "How about it? Think you can spare the time?"

"All the time you want," she promised. "But I wonder," she mused, conscious of Gus's lips coming closer. "I wonder how we'll manage in a room without a grand piano." Her teasing expression quickly became serious when she saw the look on his face, felt his arms pull her close to him.

"We'll manage," he assured her. "I have a few duets of my own in mind."

Eyes met, lips touched, bodies pressed close as they recognized the truth of what they meant to each other, what they could be together. Madeline knew this was only a beginning—and with Gus there would always be new beginnings—but the forbidden melody she had sought to deny herself had burst into sweet, sweet music.

YOU'LL BE SWEPT AWAY WITH SILHOUETTE DESIRE

$1.95 each

11 ☐ James	37 ☐ James	63 ☐ Dee	89 ☐ Ross
12 ☐ Palmer	38 ☐ Douglass	64 ☐ Milan	90 ☐ Roszel
13 ☐ Wallace	39 ☐ Monet	65 ☐ Allison	91 ☐ Browning
14 ☐ Valley	40 ☐ Mallory	66 ☐ Langtry	92 ☐ Carey
15 ☐ Vernon	41 ☐ St. Claire	67 ☐ James	93 ☐ Berk
16 ☐ Major	42 ☐ Stewart	68 ☐ Browning	94 ☐ Robbins
17 ☐ Simms	43 ☐ Simms	69 ☐ Carey	95 ☐ Summers
18 ☐ Ross	44 ☐ West	70 ☐ Victor	96 ☐ Milan
19 ☐ James	45 ☐ Clay	71 ☐ Joyce	97 ☐ James
20 ☐ Allison	46 ☐ Chance	72 ☐ Hart	98 ☐ Joyce
21 ☐ Baker	47 ☐ Michelle	73 ☐ St. Clair	99 ☐ Major
22 ☐ Durant	48 ☐ Powers	74 ☐ Douglass	100 ☐ Howard
23 ☐ Sunshine	49 ☐ James	75 ☐ McKenna	101 ☐ Morgan
24 ☐ Baxter	50 ☐ Palmer	76 ☐ Michelle	102 ☐ Palmer
25 ☐ James	51 ☐ Lind	77 ☐ Lowell	103 ☐ James
26 ☐ Palmer	52 ☐ Morgan	78 ☐ Barber	104 ☐ Chase
27 ☐ Conrad	53 ☐ Joyce	79 ☐ Simms	105 ☐ Blair
28 ☐ Lovan	54 ☐ Fulford	80 ☐ Palmer	106 ☐ Michelle
29 ☐ Michelle	55 ☐ James	81 ☐ Kennedy	107 ☐ Chance
30 ☐ Lind	56 ☐ Douglass	82 ☐ Clay	108 ☐ Gladstone
31 ☐ James	57 ☐ Michelle	83 ☐ Chance	109 ☐ Simms
32 ☐ Clay	58 ☐ Mallory	84 ☐ Powers	110 ☐ Palmer
33 ☐ Powers	59 ☐ Powers	85 ☐ James	111 ☐ Browning
34 ☐ Milan	60 ☐ Dennis	86 ☐ Malek	112 ☐ Nicole
35 ☐ Major	61 ☐ Simms	87 ☐ Michelle	113 ☐ Cresswell
36 ☐ Summers	62 ☐ Monet	88 ☐ Trevor	114 ☐ Ross

$1.95 each

115 ☐ James	134 ☐ McKenna	153 ☐ Milan	172 ☐ Stuart
116 ☐ Joyce	135 ☐ Charlton	154 ☐ Berk	173 ☐ Lee
117 ☐ Powers	136 ☐ Martel	155 ☐ Ross	174 ☐ Caimi
118 ☐ Milan	137 ☐ Ross	156 ☐ Corbett	
119 ☐ John	138 ☐ Chase	157 ☐ Palmer	
120 ☐ Clay	139 ☐ St. Claire	158 ☐ Cameron	
121 ☐ Browning	140 ☐ Joyce	159 ☐ St. George	
122 ☐ Trent	141 ☐ Morgan	160 ☐ McIntyre	
123 ☐ Paige	142 ☐ Nicole	161 ☐ Nicole	
124 ☐ St. George	143 ☐ Allison	162 ☐ Horton	
125 ☐ Caimi	144 ☐ Evans	163 ☐ James	
126 ☐ Carey	145 ☐ James	164 ☐ Gordon	
127 ☐ James	146 ☐ Knight	165 ☐ McKenna	
128 ☐ Michelle	147 ☐ Scott	166 ☐ Fitzgerald	
129 ☐ Bishop	148 ☐ Powers	167 ☐ Evans	
130 ☐ Blair	149 ☐ Galt	168 ☐ Joyce	
131 ☐ Larson	150 ☐ Simms	169 ☐ Browning	
132 ☐ McCoy	151 ☐ Major	170 ☐ Michelle	
133 ☐ Monet	152 ☐ Michelle	171 ☐ Ross	

SILHOUETTE DESIRE, Department SD/6
1230 Avenue of the Americas
New York, NY 10020

Please send me the books I have checked above. I am enclosing $_____
(please add 75¢ to cover postage and handling. NYS and NYC residents please
add appropriate sales tax). Send check or money order—no cash or C.O.D.'s
please. Allow six weeks for delivery.

NAME_____

ADDRESS_____

CITY_____ STATE/ZIP_____

Silhouette Desire